THE FINITE

The Finite

Kit Power

Black Shuck Books
www.blackshuckbooks.co.uk

First published in Great Britain in 2019 by Black Shuck Books

978-1-913038-35-9

This one's for Scarlet. Thank you.
I've loved every second of being your dad.
It's all for you.

1

My daughter's screams woke me. "Daddy Luke! Daddy Luke!"

I remember looking over at the empty patch of bed, where 'Daddy Luke' would normally be sleeping. I remember cursing him for not being here, for that bastard overnight training course taking him to London. Away from us.

"Daddy Luke!"

Fuck off, kid, you're stuck with me tonight. "Daddy Rob is coming, sweetheart!"

I was already stumbling out of bed as I said that, glancing back at the digital clock display: 3:48. I remember thinking *Christ, this fucking kid. Is she trying to kill me?*

Five minutes before the end of the world, I thought that.

She didn't protest my appearance; at least there was that. Luke and I had been trying to wean her off her dependency on him, her favouritism, but it had been hard work. Stubborn kid. She wanted what she wanted. She just clung to him. It was always Daddy Luke that got the teary hugs, the midnight calls. I envied him it, but secretly, I didn't always mind. Especially at times like this.

"What's the matter, princess?"

She lay in her bed, growling rather than crying, clutching her foot. "My foot has belly ache!"

"Aw, sweetheart. This foot?"

"Yeh." She held it up for me, and I sat on the pink chair next to her bed, rubbing it. Poor kid – growing pains were really getting bad lately. I looked at her clock as my thumbs started to move gently over the soles of her feet.

3:50

"It hurts, Daddy Rob."

"I know sweetheart, I'm sorry. Does this help?"

"Yeh."

"Okay."

I yawned, hard enough to make my jaw crackle a little. "It's late! So late for a little girl to be awake."

"Yeh."

"Do you need some medicine, do you think? Some Calpol?"

No reply. She was already drifting off again, eyes glazing over, lips drooping. I checked the clock again.

3:51

I looked back at her face, and I watched her eyes close, her breathing start to regulate. I started to relax the rubbing, and she groaned and flexed her foot again.

Not so fast, Daddy Rob.

I let out a deep sigh, and carried on rubbing my daughter's foot. I remember feeling pretty pissed off. Resentful of Luke's absence and just achingly tired. Thinking about the school run in the morning and having to get to the office afterwards. *Picked a bad day to give up coffee,* I thought, smiling to myself in the dark. Staring at the glowing green digits of the clock without really looking. Listening to the muffled rattling of the rain against the double glazing.

How long have I been doing this?

3:52 became 3:53. I gradually reduced the pressure on my daughter's foot, watching her face for any sign of stirring.

Daylight flooded the room.

My head snapped round to the window, expecting to see a helicopter or something. Instead, I saw a white light on the horizon, so bright it hurt my eyes.

It was the end of the world.

I felt my stomach drop, a bitter taste in the back of my throat. I noticed the clock had gone out.

"Daddy Rob..."

I flung myself onto the bed, covering her body with mine. She started to squeal with shock, but her cry was obliterated by the sound of breaking glass as the window shattered. I felt the whole room under us *lurch* forward, as if pushed by a giant. There was a blast of intense heat across the back of my bare legs. I yelled out, and tried to tuck them under her duvet. She'd stopped screaming, and I could feel her hot, damp breath on my chest, soaking through my T-shirt. She was panting, but not struggling. Too scared to, maybe.

The heatwave passed quickly, and the light slowly faded. I held my daughter tight and stroked her hair, whispering to her.

"It's okay, baby girl, it's okay, it'll all be over in a minute..."

As the intense brightness faded, the room fell into pitch darkness. The light from the bathroom was out. So were the streetlights outside the window.

"Daddy's got you, you're okay."

All was black.

2

So I'm Robert. Rob Andrews. And I'm dead.

Likely, I've been dead for some time, in fact. If someone is reading this, it's going to be decades from now.

Now.

Now is me sitting here, typing this. As I type, my daughter is lying next to me, in my bed. The empty windows are covered by the mattress from the spare room, but it's still cool, so Charley is wrapped up, blankets and the duvet, oblivious to the soft clacking of the keyboard.

I'm going to have to be quick. I've got this battery and one spare, so that gives me, what? 8-10 hours of typing time? About that, I think. I turned off the WiFi, turned the power settings to maximum eco, but even so, it's a juice-hungry laptop.

Okay. So this is today.

3

Eventually, Charley whispers to me in the dark.

"What's happening, Daddy Rob?"

"There's been an explosion." The pain in my legs is bad, but it's nothing compared to the feeling in my stomach. My gut is churning, and I can feel sweat popping all over my back, my face.

"Is that what broke the window?"

"Yes, sweetheart." The darkness is total. Absolute. I close my eyes anyway, trying to picture the layout of her room in my mind. The bedside table with the clock and the lamp, on the other side, her bookcase, wardrobe.

"What blew up?"

"I don't know." Which is true, but I'm pretty sure, given the direction and size of the explosion, that it was London.

I think Luke's name, but push it back down before I can picture his face. No time for that shit.

What to do? That's the question.

The rain is still coming down, the kind of summer shower that's a drag during the day, but normally comforting at night, as it drums against the walls and roof and windows of your house and you lie, snug and safe and warm and dry. Soothing.

Not so much when you can hear the raindrops landing *inside* the room.

"Is that why the lights went out?"

"I think so, yeah." EMP, or just grid disruption? My mind's running back through all those CND horror pamphlets and books I inhaled in my 20s, megatons and blast radius, psi circles and rem per hour and fallout...

"When will they come back on?"

My mind is still trying to run away, trying to calculate, like the maths problem from hell. *If a nuclear warhead detonates in or over London, and the explosion is powerful enough to shatter windows and sway houses in Milton Keynes, how long is a five-year-old girl likely to survive the resulting radiation poisoning; and, for extra marks, after how many days will she start vomiting blood?*

"When will they come back on? Daddy Rob?"

I take a deep breath. I move slowly, sliding to one side a little, but still covering most of her with my larger frame. I place my head on her pillow and talk softly, directly into her ear.

"I don't know, sweetheart. Probably not tonight."

"You mean it's going to be dark all night?"

"Yes, I think so." *And the rest.*

"I don't like the dark! I can't sleep in the dark!"

"Sweetheart..." She's getting riled now, that stubborn, angry tone entering her voice.

"No! Daddy Rob..."

"Listen, Charley..."

"No, I can't sleep in the dark, I can't..."

"I will stay with you! I'll stay with you, okay?"

That shuts her up for a second. She's very occasionally asked me to stay with her after story time – more often the proposition has gone to Daddy Luke – but we've both been firm about saying no. She needs to...

She *needed* to be okay about sleeping by herself. Now, though? *Fuck it.*

"All night?"

"Until the morning, yeah." I stroke her hair back from her forehead, then kiss her. "Okay? Daddy Rob will stay here with you, okay? Cuddle up and keep you warm until the morning. Keep you safe."

She curls up into herself at this, delighted. "I love you, Daddy Rob."

I smile next to her, honestly touched, for a split second removed from the circumstance and just glowing.

"I mean, I love Daddy Luke too..."

"I know you do, darling. So do I." I feel a lump riding in my throat at that last, but I don't think it makes it into my voice. "Go to sleep now, okay?"

"Okay. Thank you for staying with me, Daddy Rob."

It's far too much. I kiss her again and hug her tight – what she calls with delight 'a big squeezy' –

and then settle next to her, still covering as much of her body as I can with my own; partly as warming blanket, partly as shield.

I think about the layout of the room again. I'm pretty sure I could navigate out into the hall, maybe even down the stairs... but there's problems with that. For one, even if I did, I don't know where the torches are. Not a clue. For another, I'd have to leave her behind, and she'd freak out completely.

And the reason I'd have to leave her behind is because we're both barefoot, and there's broken glass all over the floor from the window. *And I am no Bruce Willis,* I think. I smile to myself in the dark, and feel the smile twist as the tears threaten to come. I choke them down as best I can,

I don't want to wake her.

4

Sorry for the present tense. I know it's confusing. I'm not much of a writer. But it's how I remember it, you see. It's all still so fresh. And I want you to see it, to feel it, the way I did. I want, as much as I can, for you to feel it as though it were happening, not as something past.

I don't want to think about being past. About *her* as past.

I'm not ready for that.

5

I lie in the dark for a while, trying to think. To work things out. My thoughts become circular: I start by trying to think about a way to get a light source, cursing myself for leaving my phone on the bedside cabinet charging. Then I try and remember if the torch is under the stairs or in the jumble drawer in the kitchen, if we have candles in that same drawer, anything to light them with, and thoughts of light remind me of the flash I saw outside the window, brighter than daylight (I was lucky not to have been blinded, I think) and the heat from that blast, the burns on the back of my legs and what they probably mean, especially coupled with the rain that has fallen steadily since the blast, and my only question is how big a dose we took, how powerful, and I'm trying to feel like there could be a chance, if we get medical treatment soon, but the fire in my legs and the heat and force of the blast tell me that's a fool's hope, that there's no medical help coming, not with enough medicine for a town this size, and the truth is, the dose is almost certainly untreatable, I'd know more if only I could see the damage to my legs... and the cycle starts again.

Time is slippery now, the only constant my

daughter's hot breath against my chest. My mind tries to move to her, or to Luke, and I pull it back to the floor and the darkness and the light, afraid, desperately scared of what will happen if I allow myself to start really facing them. It's shock, sure, and I have no idea how much time has passed before light flickers into the bedroom, pale, blue, bright, and a familiar voice yells "Rob? Luke? Anyone home?"

It's Pete, of Pete and Sharon fame. My neighbours.

"Pete!"

Charley stirs. I think about walking down the mattress to get close to the window, but I'm worried about the glass again. I settle for sitting up, smoothing the duvet back over her, tucking her in. The rain has cooled the air, but it's not actually cold.

"Rob?"

"Yeah."

"Are you and Luke okay? Charley?"

"I... Charley and me are okay, yeah. We're... stuck, actually. In her room. There's glass all over the floor and it's pitch black..."

"Right! Right. Want me to come up? I'm... erm, the fence is down, which is how I got in the garden – I thought I'd better have a look and see if everything was okay, you know..."

"You okay? Sharon?"

“She’s fine, yeah, we’re on the other side of the house, so the window blew out rather than in. Bloody scary moment, but we’re alright. She’s got the gas stove out, she’s making a cuppa now. D’you want me to come in? Your patio doors are broken, I could get through...”

“Would you?”

“Of course, yeah! No problem. You in the back room?”

“Yeah, me and Charley.”

“Okay, see you shortly.”

I hear footsteps, first squelching, then sploshing, then crunching as he approaches the house. I feel my way back to Charley and shake her. She grumbles – not speaking, just a noise in her throat.

“Charley, sweetheart, you have to wake up.”

“Muuuuuuuuuuhh”

“Charley. Charley.”

“Don’ wanna...”

“Come on, baby girl, I know you don’t want to, but you need to wake up now.

“Daddy Rob...”

I hear the door open as bright torchlight stabs into my eyes, and this time Charley and I groan as one, involuntarily.

The light plays over the floor. There’s glass all over the carpet, the pink chair, which is now soaked with rain water. The glass twinkles dully. Overlaid on that is a fine layer of dark grey-brown dust. It coats the floor, the duvet, my own arms and body. I see it in Charley's hair. My stomach sinks, my worst fears realised.

"Well, THIS is a bit of a mess, isn't it?"

Outside, the rain hammers down. Relentless.

6

We're in Pete and Sharon's house. I've never been in here before.

It's kind of a revelation.

There's a lot of mirrors. Like, a disconcerting amount. Vintage, or copies of same – Pepsi, Esso, Marilyn, Elvis. We sit in the living room, and my eyes keep getting drawn to the (please let it be fake) huge oil painting of a racehorse over the mantelpiece, in a heavy wooden frame. The zebra print rug (!) that covers most of the living room floor. The porcelain knick-knacks that seem to cover every available flat surface. The cumulative effect is one of profoundly irritating distraction – there's always something in the corner of your eye screaming for your attention.

The light source doesn't help – maybe a dozen tea lights on a coffee table in the centre of the rug, the flames flickering every time anybody stands up or sits down, sending reflections across all the damn mirrors and porcelain like a geriatric glitter ball.

I'm being spoken to.

"Sorry?"

"How's the tea? Is it okay?"

I look down at the not-quite warm enough cup of what appears to be grey dishwater. I take a sip. It tastes about as bad as it looks, albeit sweeter. "Lovely, thanks."

I give Sharon a smile, which she returns automatically. It's a sad, distracted thing, but better than nothing.

"So..." says Pete, and I gratefully drag my eyes away from his wife's made up face and leopard print silk dressing gown and back to his bloodshot blue eyes under bushy grey brows "...you think it was London?"

I take him in, try to. His grey hair, even at four in the morning, combed in regimented lines back from his forehead. His perma-tan spectacularly failing to hide the paleness around his eyes and lips, or the high colour on his cheekbones, almost like rouge. Those eyes – watery, but unwavering.

I take another sip of dishwater to buy some time, but it doesn't help much, and I'm left with "I think so, yeah."

He puffs his cheeks out, holds the pose for a second, then *poooofs* the air out in a sigh, sending sparkle lights across my field of vision. He looks old. I mean, he *is* old, they both are, in their seventies at least, but with the tans and the carefully selected wardrobe and so on, they normally make a good fist of looking... not young, but alert, wiry. Healthy.

Not tonight. I guess 4am and crisis have a way of reasserting the age thing.

"Russians, do you think? Or that American lunatic, even?"

Part of me wants to laugh. I mean, what could it possibly matter? But then I look down at Charley, sacked out on the leather sofa next to me under a mountain of blankets. *Be kind,* says Luke in my mind, as he often would in person, and I shy away from that train of thought in a hurry, but it centres me. Another sip of mud, then

"I don't know, obviously, but I doubt it. If it was them, there'd be more bombs, I think. A lot more. I mean, it could have been an accident, I suppose. Anything's possible. But I doubt it."

He's nodding soberly as I stumble my way through my thoughts, taking it in.

"So you think it's the... you know... whachercallem... Jihaddies?"

I think about that for a second.

"If I was guessing, yes. It must have been a warhead, the size of the blast... I mean, if that was London and it was this big this far out, that's a huge device, has to be a warhead..." I realise I'm painfully close to rambling, talking too fast, but can't seem to help it. "So, so it's probably a stolen device, or bought, you know, black market, Russia's been a mess since forever, huge arsenal, it only takes one..."

He's nodding again, looking a little paler.

"I mean, I'm just guessing. Like I said, could be a misfire, I suppose."

"You don't think it was a meltdown, maybe? Like Chernobyl?" He nods at Sharon. "We thought..."

I glance back at her, and see something awful in her face. Sadness and fear, mixing to make desperation. I swallow hard before answering.

"I... it's possible, of course, but it looked like a detonation to me." My mind travels back to the brightness of the first flash, the burns on the back of my calves that are still throbbing, just starting to itch as well as hurt, and the dust coating the interior of my little girl's bedroom. Most of all, that dust. On the floor, and in the rain, staining the drops brown as they ran down the waterproofs I threw over myself and Charley as I carried her across the lawn into my neighbours' garden. If it was London, only a warhead would get the blast and debris to us that quickly. Which means the rem count in the fallout that is soaking into the ground outside, and that is coating my daughter's room – that we inhaled and lay under for at least thirty minutes before Pete and his torch came to the rescue – is more than enough to kill us all.

I look back at the sleeping bundle next to me, and completely miss the next question.

"Sorry?"

"I said, how do you know all this?" It's Sharon talking, and I turn to look at her.

"Erm, well, I don't know anything, really. But I was in CND for a few years, and I read a lot about the subject back then. I mean, I imagine I'm out of date, there's got to have been... developments, technological, what have you, but..."

"...but you think...?"

"...Yeah."

We sit in silence, I sip mud. My mind pulls me back to Charley, and I place a hand gently on the blankets covering her, feeling the rise and fall of her breath.

I feel tears threaten then.

"Okay, so what now?"

I look up at Pete. His tone is almost conversational, but there's a desperate hunger in his eyes.

"Well, I'd start with a radio. If it... if it's just London, there should be some broadcast from elsewhere..."

"Manchester!" His face brightens.

"Well, yes, possibly..."

"Yeah, with the BBC move from London. Of course. We've got one in the shower, I'll just..." He gets up slowly, carefully, and heads out of the living room.

I look at Sharon. She smiles, but it looks like an effort. She's clearly terrified.

"What do you think happens next?" There are

questions behind the question, and panic just under the surface, and the obvious answer feels… unhelpful.

Be kind.

"At a guess, I'd say there'll be an evacuation."

Her eyebrows shoot up. "Really?"

"Look, honestly, I don't know any more than you, I'm just guessing, but…"

"No, no, I understand…"

"…hopefully the radio will tell us more…"

"My dad was an evacuee, you know. During the war."

It's uncomfortable, almost painful, this reaching for something relatable, something grounding. Part of me wants to laugh, but I'm not remotely amused.

Be kind.

"Really?"

"Oh, yes, he…"

"Got it! Got it. Nothing yet though, just a test bleep at the moment, but…" The radio is moulded yellow plastic, clearly designed to be waterproof, with Homer Simpson on the side.

7

Shit, I'm rambling. Sorry, sorry. Trying to get it all, but that's pointless. Time's a'wasting, and so is my battery life. Must type faster. Think faster.

8

We sat together in the living room until dawn. Small talk died quickly, and we all took to staring at the radio, willing it to do something more than beep at us. I remember shutting my eyes a few times, trying to rest; my head was swimming with thoughts that threatened to become dreams, but something kept making me snap awake. I'd thought about trying to find a way to take Charley and go back to the house, but they clearly expected me to feel as mesmerised by the radio as they were, and with my daughter sleeping, I just couldn't muster the energy to break through the social pressure.

Cars drove by infrequently, but often enough to provide another barrier to sleep. I wondered where they thought they were going, and where they were *really* going. It apparently hadn't occurred to Pete or Sharon to try and leave. Waiting for orders, I supposed. I wished the drivers and passengers well, but I was afraid for them.

I was just starting to notice a creeping greyness around the edges of the room, the dawn twilight, when the radio started talking. I can't remember the whole message, but the gist was: stay indoors, conserve water, help is on the way. I wondered about that last part.

"Nothing about evacuation." It wasn't exactly an accusation from Sharon, but it wasn't far off either.

"It's a general broadcast. Probably a recording. Still, it's a good sign. The infrastructure's in place. Right?" Pete glanced at me with that last, a kind of gentle appeal in his eyes.

"Absolutely..."

"Preserve water? Are the taps not working? I just used the water in the kettle for the tea, didn't think to check..." Her voice trailed off.

Fear was suddenly in the room with us all, close, oppressive. I could feel it, a sinking in my stomach. I thought about Luke, and his jogging obsession – about the crate of 'sport' water bottles. How many?

"Even if it does run, do you suppose it's safe?" Pete, looking to me again. I took a second to resent it, the churning in my gut growing worse, the beginnings of a sleep deprivation headache lurking behind my eyes.

"I... I wouldn't. Don't know where the reservoir is for us, but if there's fallout... can't be filtered for..."

Nods all round.

"What a pickle. Good job we've got plenty of beer in the shed. Be like the old days! They used to drink beer all the time, didn't they, back in the old days..."

His words had started to fade. I felt sweat on my

forehead, the taste of the horrid tea rising in the back of my throat. I felt dizzy, and placed a hand on Charley's huddled form. So still.

"...you okay? You've gone awfully pale..."

I closed my eyes, tight, screwing my face up, then opened them wide. The light felt too bright.

"I'm fine, I just..."

But I wasn't fine. My gut was roiling now, threatening mutiny, sweat all over my skin. I rubbed my hand over Charley, as much for my comfort as hers, and breathed deep, trying to get myself under control.

"...you feel sick? Sharon, fetch a bag..."

I was going to puke, that was clear now. I thought about standing up, actually started to put my weight on the hand that was resting on my daughter. I looked over at her then. Just a child-shaped lump under a blanket.

I stared at the lump, hand on her side.

It didn't move. At all.

She wasn't breathing.

9

The shock hit me like a physical thing. I shuddered, the feeling rippling down my spine. I grabbed a fistful of the blanket and yanked it, lurching to my feet as I did so.

It took me more effort than it should have done, and panic made me overcompensate, and her body spun as she fell off the couch. She hit the ground limp – no attempt to break her fall, no indication she'd known she *was* falling.

Her skin was so white. Almost translucent. I felt vomit rise in my throat again.

"Rob, what...?" It's Pete.

"She's not breathing." Even as I said it, I fell to my knees, scooping her into my arms. I looked at her face as her head lolled back. She was still warm – too warm – but her eyes were shut, her neck slack. I felt terror rising then, threatening to overwhelm everything, but I forced it back down. I pulled her chin down.

The smell of vomit hit me immediately, making my eyes water, but I barely noticed. I turned her over so her head was facing the ground. I put my fingers into her mouth, clawing at the soft pulp I found there, shaking her as I did so, some half-assed heimlich. I scooped, went back in, scooped some more, fingerfuls of her stomach contents splattering onto the carpet. After the second scoop it started flowing on its own, I could feel it running past my fingers, pouring out of her. I put my hand back on her chin, holding her mouth open, feeling the warm fluid running over my fingers, my mind just repeating one word over and over again, *breathe, breathe, breathe, breathe, breathe...*

And then she did. It was ragged, and as soon as she started, she coughed, gagged, spat, coughed some more. Her whole body spasmed in my grip, and she heaved in breath and choked out vomit and spit. I placed my face on her back, letting her feel my breath, trying to give comfort.

"It's okay, it's okay..."

Her coughing gradually dissolved into sobbing. I can't remember ever being so happy to hear my daughter crying. I pulled my head back. I saw how my own tears had made an impression of my face on the back of her pajama top.

A shudder ran through me, and I turned my head and puked, ejecting the foul tea and the last of the previous evening's meal in one hot stream. It washed over the black and white rug like a polluted tidal wave, lapping against Pete's blue slippers.

I looked up at him. His face was a mask of surprise so total it was almost comical.

"Sorry," I croaked.

Then his face swam before my eyes, and I blacked out.

10

I wasn't out for long – just a few seconds, Pete said. Coming round was rough, I know that. My throat and nose felt coated with bitterness and stomach acid, and my head was pounding with my pulse.

I had a blessed couple of seconds of total disorientation, when my mind was trying to make sense of a rug that was black and white and puked all over, and then I remembered. Sitting up nearly made me black out again, but I clung on to the side of the coffee table until my vision cleared.

Charley was okay. Shivering, sweaty, and the poor kid had some sick in her hair – hers or mine, I couldn't tell for sure – but she was awake. She sat cross legged on the floor, the duvet back around her shoulders. Shivering.

"I don't feel well, Daddy Rob."

Her eyes were pink from the vomiting, her cheeks wet from crying, but her gaze was steady.

"Me either, sweet pea."

"I want to go home."

"Me too."

"Are you sure?" Pete looked worried, but I thought I saw a sneaky relief too – like when the party guest you realise has had too much to drink announces he's leaving early.

"Yeah, I think it's best, we've got... medicine at home," I looked at Charley, tried a wink. "How about some pink medicine, kiddo? Settle your stomach?"

"Yeh. Can you carry me?"

"Of course I can" I said, with far more confidence than I was feeling. Getting her up from the floor was the hardest part, but she helped me out, clinging on with her legs. Sharon and Pete kept asking if we were sure as they led us to the back door, and I struggled with the breath to tell them it was fine. "Just let us know if the message on the radio changes, okay?"

"Of course we will, yeah. We'll pop in a bit later and check on you, okay?"

"That'd be good Pete, yes, thanks." I wondered if they'd be able to, how long it'd be before the sickness hit them. I thought again about the dust, coating the inside of her room. They had some on the kitchen floor, but otherwise their house was relatively clear. Not having the rear patio doors must have helped. I thought for a second about how much they'd cost us to fit, my insistence on having natural light in our living room, Luke's acquiescence, and tears came close again.

Pete insisted on walking us back to the house, in through the shattered door. I couldn't conceal my sigh of relief as I put Charley down on the sofa. She was already halfway asleep. I needed to get some medicine down her.

Pete hovered. I decided to break the silence.

“Listen, I’m so sorry about that, your rug...”

“No, no, don’t be silly, just glad the little one is okay. You gave us quite a scare there, didn’t you?” I saw her blue eyes flash up to his face, mistrustful. She nodded once, not smiling.

“Yeah. Still, all okay now, home safe, eh?” His eyes wandered around the room as he spoke, taking in the shattered windows, the scattered newspapers, blown from the pile on the floor all over the room by the blast.

“Yes, all safe.” He made eye contact with me, hesitated, then spoke. “Rob, can I...?” He nodded back in the direction of the garden. I ached – throat, stomach, head, and it was starting to spread to my arms too. I needed rest, and so did my little girl. Still...

Be kind.

I wrapped Charley up carefully, kissed her forehead. “Back in a second, sweetheart. Try and rest.”

I walked with Pete over to the patio doors. The rain had stopped, and the outside temperature was rising.

He nodded back, eyes flicking to the sofa where my daughter lay.

"Is she... she'll be okay now, you think?"

"I hope so, yes." *Until she isn't.* But I wasn't going there – not with Pete. "She just needs to get some medicine down her, get her stomach settled. She'll be okay in a day or two." *Probably. For a while, anyway.*

"And you, uh..."

I tried a smile. Don't know how it looked, but it didn't feel good. "The same. Like a stomach bug."

He nodded, those watery blue eyes meeting mine, darting away, coming back. He had something to say, that was clear, but I just couldn't bring myself to push him. Not after puking on his rug. Would have felt impolite.

Eventually, he spoke. "So... so, d'you think we'll get sick too? Sharon and I, I mean?"

So that's what this is about. What to say, that was the problem. I opted for almost-not-lying.

"Well, that depends on how much fallout made it into your house. Possibly, possibly not. If you do, it'll just be like a stomach upset, you should get better."

"Right, right." He looked worried, scared even, away from his wife, without someone to have to act brave for. "What... Can they treat it, or...?"

"It's not like that, exactly. But you should get better..."

"Couple of days?"

"Yeah."

"Like a tummy bug?"

"Yeah. Like that."

He looked at me for a long time after that, and I thought he was going to say something else, but instead he just said "Okay."

He agreed again to come and check on us later, and let us know if the radio message changed (no battery powered wireless for us, Luke's love of gadgets had seen to that; nothing but the best mains-fed digital devices, all just lumps of expensive, useless plastic now) we shook hands, his skin leathery, but the grip dry and firm, and then he left us.

I could already feel the nausea starting to rise again when I turned back to Charley, but I had work to do, so I tried to think of other things. She was groggy, but I got some Calpol down her – noting the half a bottle we had left, already thinking about rations, if it would be enough, how long she'd feel like this – then carried her up to my bedroom. I made sure she was propped on her side and got a couple of bowls from under the sink – one for her, one for me. Even with empty stomachs, I thought it would be best to have somewhere to be sick into, keep it contained. She was asleep by the time I went back into the room, which I thought was, on balance, good – it would give the medicine time to work, hopefully soothe her head and throat and stomach. They must be hurting, because mine were, even though I could feel a crushing fatigue setting in just from going up and down the stairs. Luckily my room had a lot less damage, the windows blown out rather than in as the blast had passed through the house, and none of that dust. I shut her bedroom door to prevent the draft carrying it further into the house, though I noticed the footprints we'd left in the hall during our early-hours exodus with a kind of dull dismay.

The temperature was already starting to rise, the sunlight sending rays through the clouds. I dragged the mattress from the spare room and placed it loosely in the window frame, shading the bed.

And that's where I am now. Outside the sun has climbed to close to overhead. My daughter is still asleep next to me. She's woken once to throw up, and sipped some water down before falling back to sleep. I've dozed in between dry heaves, dreams sweaty, incoherent, until I remembered this laptop. I thought the EMP must have knocked it out, but no. Either we're too far out, or it doesn't affect devices that aren't switched on. No internet to check it either way. Not anymore.

I really don't know why I'm doing this. It's utterly pointless, counterproductive even. I should just be resting. Saving my strength. I'm going to need it, over the next week or two. But I look at Charley sleeping, and I look at the photo of Luke and I on the wall, and I want you to know that we're real, and that we exist. Existed.

I've used up 50% of my battery power already. What's that give me, 6 more hours, with the spare pack?

Fuck.

Fuck it, enough for one day.

11

So today the soldiers came.

The rest of the previous day passed in a blur – a sweaty daze that stank of stomach acid and bile and pounded in time with my heart. Pete did call back round, once, in the afternoon, but when he caught the smell and sight of us, he didn't stay long. I'd emptied both Charley's bowl and my own down the sink in the bathroom – I hadn't put them down the toilet, I had that much presence of mind, at least – but with no way to rinse them, they retained that bitter smell. Charley had also thrown up into the bed at one point – just water, really, all food long gone from her stomach – and I'd covered it with a towel. I was acutely conscious that we had one clean set of sheets left, and I didn't want to use them until we were through this.

The day was slow to die, and the blood-red of the sunset had me wondering if I was hallucinating. I'd been getting the shakes intermittently, my stomach muscles felt rubbery and sore from all the heaving, and my bones ached, but that last didn't feel like a temperature, more like a reaction to the constant throwing up. I made Charley drink sips of water now and then, when she surfaced, and she felt bad enough that she didn't really argue, even though, like me, it generally didn't stay down for long. I tried to time the Calpol doses for when she was falling asleep – the first time I got it wrong and she puked it back up, but the second time I got lucky and she stayed under.

I'd tried Ibuprofen tablets for me but they'd come back up almost at once – my throat was too raw. So I just rode the cramps out as best I could and tried to sleep.

The night didn't last long. Soon enough, the sun was prickling my closed eyes, warming the room. I'd used pillows to prop Charley on her side as she'd slept, and I removed a layer of blankets to stop her getting too warm – it was shaping up to be another scorcher.

That was when I heard the rumbling of the trucks.

There were a lot of them, heading down the main road behind the house. I didn't want to go to the back rooms to try and see; the tree cover hid the road, and there was the broken glass and dust. Instead, I peered around the mattress in the window and gazed into the street.

The trucks reached the crossroads at the top of the street – big personnel carriers, army green and camo. They peeled off, two per street. They both stopped on the other side of the road. I saw two figures jump out of the first truck. I saw the second one was empty.

More figures were appearing from the first truck now, walking down the street, fanning out. I saw them knocking on the door of the house opposite ours, and felt a jolt.

Evacuation.

I looked back at Charley. No time to wake her, to try and explain. No time at all, probably. I ran down the stairs, through the living room and out the shattered doors, into my neighbours' garden.

As I reached the back door, Pete was just heading out, and he reared back in shock. He looked paler than he had yesterday, and more tired. On the plus side, he was dressed.

"Rob! Blimey..."

"Sorry! Sorry, I was just..."

"The soldiers? Yes! Evacuation, you think?"

"I do, yeah..."

"Well, that's good, isn't it? Probably got treatment centres set up, emergency hospitals, that sort of thing, I expect..."

"Probably, yeah. Listen, Pete..."

I hated cutting him off – I could see he was excited, relieved. But I had to. Time was running out.

"What is it?" His smile faded from his face as he took in my expression. I was sorry to see it go.

"We're not leaving. Charley and I, I mean."

Pete's brow furrowed. "Why not?"

And here it was. I looked into his eyes, willing him to understand.

"I'm worried that Luke might come back and not know where we are. Not be able to find us. And Charley is scared. I don't want to take her out of her home." The lie felt pitiful, desperate, as it left my lips. Of course Luke's not fucking coming back. None of us are. Would he see the truth behind it, understand my real reason for wanting, needing to stay? Would he understand my desperation? Enough, too much?

Pete nodded, eyes not leaving mine. His face was very grave.

"So you're... She's still not well?"

"No, she isn't. And as I said, I don't want..."

"...Yeah, no, of course, I understand..." He nodded, breaking eye contact. His eyes travelled over the wall of his house. They looked damp to me, and I suddenly felt tears stinging in my own eyes.

"Listen, Pete..."

"Tell you what, here."

He rummaged in his pocket and pulled out a keyring. He held it out to me.

"Here you go. Keep an eye on the place for us, would you? And, you know, help yourself to... you know, if you need anything..."

His voice started to crack on that last, and he swallowed suddenly and looked down at the ground. I felt an incredible urge to hug him, a wave of affection that rolled through me, warming me up. I took the keys from his hand and pocketed them. "Thank you. I will."

He nodded, not looking up. We stood in silence, and I realised with mounting panic that I had no idea how to end the conversation. Too much feeling. Not enough words.

"Well..." said Pete, flapping his arms once against his side. He briefly made eye contact, and suddenly I held my hand out.

We shook. He smiled, then said "Good luck, neighbour."

"You too, Pete."

"Yeah, yeah. Hope... well, take care, okay?"

"You too. You and Sharon."

He chuckled at that, pure reflex, no humour.

"Oh, her! She'll outlast us all, no danger!"

I smiled that that. "Okay, Pete, I'd best get back..."

He waved me off. "Course, yeah. Give her a hug from me."

"I will."

We made eye contact once more, then I turned and left.

12

I ran back into the house and up the stairs, legs and back snarling in protest. Back in my room, I peered carefully out of the window. The soldiers had worked their way down the other side of the street and had crossed over, heading back towards us. I saw my neighbours assembling, milling about – some in nightclothes, some dressed. Sweat was pouring off me, the quick sprint leaving my breathing ragged and my throat tight.

"PLEASE MAKE YOUR WAY TO THE EVACUATION TRUCKS. TAKE NOTHING WITH YOU AS IT MAY BE CONTAMINATED. PLEASE LOCK YOUR HOUSES. THE TOWN IS UNDER MARTIAL LAW AND YOUR BELONGINGS WILL BE SAFE UNTIL YOU RETURN."

The people I could see looked at each other, hesitated, then started shuffling towards the trucks at the end of the street. Further down, I could see a man dragging a suitcase, arguing with a soldier. The soldier's back was to me. His body language gave nothing away, but the face of the man was flushed, anger masking fear. My gut churned. I could taste bitterness in the back of my throat.

"Daddy, what's that shouting?"

Her voice was loud, piercing. I winced at the pain in my head, and my teeth ground together. As I opened my eyes again, I saw a soldier heading towards our house.

No good.

"Shh!"

I spat the word out as I span around to face her. I could feel the anger on my face as I hissed "We have to be very, very quiet now."

I saw her face frown back. Indignant. "But why is there SHOUTING?" Her pain and confusion giving way to anger, that stubborn streak, her voice cracked and strident.

Something hammered on the front door, hard enough that I could hear it rattling in its frame.

"SHHHHHHHH!" Glaring at her, my finger pushed into my lips. No good. I saw her open her mouth again, draw breath. I moved fast, clamping my hand over her mouth, cutting off the shout of surprise. I could feel her yelling into my hand, and I leaned over her, whispering furiously into her ear.

"Shh, shhh, be quiet! Be quiet! It's not safe!"

More hammering from downstairs.

"IS THERE ANYONE HOME? THIS IS A GENERAL EVACUATION, IT'S NOT SAFE TO STAY HERE..."

She squirmed her head from side to side, eyes tearful and angry. I pushed down harder with my hand, clamping to cut off all noise. I could feel her breath from her nose, hot and fast over the back of my knuckles.

"...you HAVE to be quiet now, you HAVE to stay silent..."

"WE ARE AUTHORISED TO FORCE ENTRY!"

I felt her try and shake her head, and winced as I pushed back against it. Her tears made me feel sick, suddenly, dizzy. I leaned closer, trying to keep the edge out of my voice.

"...I'm sorry, I'm sorry, but you have to be quiet, there's a bad man at the door and if he hears us, we'll have to leave..."

"I REPEAT WE ARE..."

"...please, he might try and hurt us, we have to..."

"...AUTHORISED TO..."

"...this all about, what are you doing?"

Pete's voice, high, indignant. Not an ounce of fear.

I could have kissed him. I looked at the window, then back at Charley. Her frown was gone, but her eyes still looked angry. I leaned over again and whispered "Please, little girl, please stay quiet, I'm sorry but you have to be quiet until the men go away, okay? I'm not trying to be mean, but if they hear you, we will have to go away with them, and I don't want to, okay?" Trying to force my breathing to slow down, I released some of the pressure on her face, and she didn't push back.

At the same time, I could hear Pete below, still talking to the soldiers: "...nobody there, they're away in London for a while. We've been looking after the place for them. Come on, there's no point kicking the door down, there's nobody there."

God bless you, Pete. I thought. *God bless you and keep you.* Charley nodded at me, then held her arms out. I took my hand from her mouth, wincing at the red fingermarks on her cheek, and hugged her, and she pulled me in tight, squeezing my neck painfully. Sobbing silently.

"Okay sir. Would you mind coming with us please, you and your wife? We need to evacuate."

"Yes, of course, of course! Come on love, time to go!"

Charley's breath tickled my ear as she whispered "I'm sorry, Daddy Rob, I didn't know..."

I felt a lump rise in my throat then, but luckily I didn't have to speak back, only whisper "Shh, I'm sorry, it's okay little girl, I'm sorry, daddy's got you, you're okay, just shh, it'll all be okay..."

Willing my heart to slow down. Little by little it did. Outside, through the shattered window, I listened to the sounds of the evacuation, overlaid with the gentle sobbing of my daughter in my ear.

13

I held her a long time, letting my ears watch the street. Lots of muttered conversation, lots of feet trudging across tarmac. Eventually she released me and lay back down in our bed, but I didn't return to the window. I looked at the angry red mark on her cheek, fading now, thank God, but still visible in the shape of my fingers, and my stomach turned over again. I remembered the panic building, the anger, and the shame of it made my heart feel heavy and painful.

I stayed with her as she slipped back asleep, and she was deep enough under that even the noise of the truck engines didn't wake her when they fired up. I waited several minutes after the last one had left, almost mesmerised by the sudden silence from the outside world. For the first time since my childhood, all I could hear were birds and the breeze through the trees. It felt soothing, but also jagged and wrong, and I felt my heart-rate start to pick up again.

Eventually I risked a peek outside. Empty. The soldiers were all gone – neighbours too, as far as I could tell.

I took some deep breaths, tried to think. What

mattered now was supplies. We'd still be sick for another day or so, but after that we should feel better, for a week at least. Maybe two. So we'd need water. I'd need to inventorise Pete and Sharon's, see what they had. Also food. The freezer would probably keep things for another couple of days, maybe, but I wasn't sure if any of it would cook over that little gas burner of Sharon's. Tins, that's the ticket. See what there was, their place and ours.

The thoughts were coming in too fast, too fragmented. I felt my temper rising again, angry at feeling so miserable, so ill. I flashed on Luke – my lovely man. Eyes full of concern, before he left. "Don't forget to..."

Oh, shit.

I left Charley's side and went to the bathroom, shakes starting again, and opened the medicine cabinet. Luke was right, I always forgot to take my pills when he wasn't here, stupid, always was an anxious mess by the time he got back, no wonder...

I scanned the shelf and snatched my prescription out, dropping the cardboard box at first, then pulling out the foil pack and turning it over.

There were eleven holes, showing the white plastic underneath.

Three remained sealed.

Three pills left.

My stomach clenched, bad enough that I doubled

over with the pain, spilling the packet into the sink. I gritted my teeth against the wave of nausea and fear, willing myself not to throw up.

Three pills left.

Fucking hell, Luke, what am I going to do?

14

This is on you, Luke.

I'm back in the bedroom now, typing when I should be resting. Listening to my stomach gurgle and my little girl breathe. My little girl. No, our little girl. No, no, fuck it, YOUR little girl. She was always yours. Biology talks, doesn't it, Luke? We said it wouldn't and we said we'd treat her the same and we did but blood talks to blood and she knew all the same. Every time she was ill, every time she was scared, every fall and every boo-boo and every nightmare, it was Daddy Luke she ran too, Daddy Luke she cried out for, Daddy Luke she needed, and where the fuck are you, Daddy Luke? Because we need you now. We need you. We're sick, and we're scared, and there's no help to be had and no water in the tap and I have three pills left and I don't know what to do.

And you had to go, didn't you? Had to go off to London for your fucking training course, learning all about crowd control and urban pacification bullshit, anti-terrorism in the big smoke, and the irony is so bitter I can taste it in the back of my throat, literally, the bile is right there, burning my vocal chords and making it hard to breathe, I hate the job, and I hate you for going and leaving us and never coming back and leaving me with YOUR daughter who is sick and who I now somehow have to find a way to care for while she gets better and then worse and then...

I'm crying now, it's getting hard to see the screen.

I have got things to do. Another day or two of this shit, enough time to figure out what we've got, hopefully enough time for the evacuation to complete, then I need water. Somehow. Food, somehow.

I've only got three pills left.

Three good days.

Except, not really. Because of how they work. It's a gradual thing, the drug builds up in your system. Over time. So I'm just starting to feel jittery now because it's been, what? How long? Two days? Yes, two days. Okay. So I'm just starting to get the wobblies, and of course I'd be feeling like shit anyway, which doesn't help...

But the thing is, the first pill won't even me out, exactly – it might take the edge off, but I've still got another day of feeling a bit like this, then maybe two clear days, maybe three as the last pill lingers, and then...

I can feel the panic rising as I sit here. I can't go back to being that person. I CAN'T. It isn't FAIR.

15

Anxiety.

Just anxiety.

That's all.

Your heart is constantly racing, your teeth constantly on edge. You grind them in your sleep and wake up with a sore jaw. You feel run down all the time, exhausted, like you're not sleeping at all, like you're slipping from sleeping nightmare to waking nightmare, in some kind of circle of purgatory. Everything is painful. Light stabs your eyes, making your brain throb sickly. All noise, all sound, music, speech, laughter, it's all drilling into your head, causing pain, anger. Eating becomes just another chore, shovelling fuel into an unsettled stomach. Nausea becomes a constant companion, a smiling yellow-skinned child that sits on your stomach every time you smell food, drenching you in its rotten bitter breath as it laughs and your gut twists.

It doesn't start like that, of course. It comes on gradual. Headaches you can't shift. Fatigue. The days just get a little harder, the lure of the bed that little bit more seductive. You keep telling yourself you're just a bit tired, a bit run down. It's the job, it's the hours, it's the demanding kid, it's the housework, that's all, just need to get a bit more sleep, a bit more rest. But it sneaks up on you. You find yourself worrying about everything. The noise the car makes. The tone of your husband's snoring. The mole on your arm. It's all needles, sticking you, tricking you. You can't relax. You spend all day tired and then lie there in bed with the light out, mind going over and over all the things you forgot to remember, all the things you don't know, and when you sleep the dreams are dark and scary and you wake up too early and can't get back, and meanwhile the hamster wheel of your mind just rolls and rolls...

And you do, you try and talk about it, but your man doesn't understand, he tries to fix it, every issue you raise, it's barely out your mouth before he's telling you how to make it better, and he's trying but he just doesn't UNDERSTAND, he doesn't GET IT, and you talk less and hug less and kiss less and fuck less, and you feel colder and hotter and more and more wretched until one day you're driving the car with your daughter in the back and you suddenly feel like you're having a heart attack, like you can't breathe, and you pull over and you call an ambulance and you try and tell your daughter it's okay, that Daddy Rob is okay, but you're scared and she can see you're scared and she's screaming at you in the car seat and you can't reach around to get her out, she's screaming and screaming and getting further and further away...

And then you wake up in a hospital bed, and everyone is there, and everyone is concerned, and it should make you feel better but it doesn't, somehow, and then after all the tests the Doctor takes you into a room and says

"Okay, Mr. Hartwell, we've run all the tests, and the good news is, your heart is fine, your body is fine, you haven't had a heart attack or a stroke, okay?"

And he smiles, kindly, and you try and smile back but it's weak so you give up and say

"So what's wrong with me? Because it felt so horrible, so scary..."

And he frowns, carefully, and he leans in, and he says

"Mr. Hartwell, are you suffering from anxiety or stress?"

And that's all it is. Just anxiety. Just a panic attack. Just stress.

Nothing really wrong with you.

And oh, the shame of that – all that drama over nothing, all those professionals, all that concern, your daughter strapped in and hysterical... all over just not being able to deal with the day to day, just a failure to fucking COPE.

And a single tiny pill to fix it all. You're sceptical

at first, but also scared – real or not, the panic attack felt like the end of everything, and you don't want to do it again. And there's work to consider – sure, they *say* take all the time you need, come back when you're well, on and on, but stress is a black mark, total barrier to further promotion – shows you can't hack it, can't take pressure. No good. No good at all. And it's not like you're saving the world or working in the city for some high pressure bank – it's just a fucking call centre management position, just a team of forty that can raise to sixty when the work is really lumpy, and sure, that's a lot to manage, but it's not the kind of job where you end up mopping up blood on a regular basis, and that just makes the failure to cope more humiliating.

So you take the little pill, once a day as directed, and little by little things start to come back into focus. You remember how to smile, and how to laugh, and you reconnect with people and the world, and by the time your sign-off period is up, you're ready to get back to it, and so you do.

And as long as you remember to take the pill, things are fine.

And when you forget, you're fine for a couple of days, and then the jitters start, your fuse shortens at home and your attention span starts to fade at work, and eventually Luke says to you 'Did you remember to take your pill?'

It's like you're still here, Luke. I know you're not. I know it was London, and if it was big enough to break glass here, it was big enough to melt concrete where you were. I know that there's never going to be a grave for you, beyond the memorial that your crater will no doubt become. Not a place that anyone will be able to visit, of course. Maybe they'll do flyovers. Maybe they'll build a monument somewhere else. A wall of names. Have to be a fucking big wall.

I'm crying, trying to do it quietly. I'm going to have to get up off this bathroom floor soon. In a minute, I'm going to have to get back into the bedroom and see how my little girl is doing. Start taking stock, figuring out how much we have, and what our next move is.

In a minute.

16

It's later now, evening. A colder one tonight. I've piled clothes, jumpers, blankets over Charley, and she's sleeping huddled under it all like a bear cub hibernating. She's already starting to bounce back – hasn't been sick in hours, is complaining about hunger. I gave her some dry bread – we've got half a loaf in the cupboard, and another full loaf slowly defrosting in the freezer – and she ate it eagerly. Going to have to get something more substantial down her in the morning.

Talking of which, I did the inventory as best I could, next door and our place. Foodwise, we're doing okay, actually. Next door were tinned food nuts, it turns out, and they liked to buy in bulk. I shudder to think what all those canned meals must have been like for the pair of them, but there were two kitchen cupboards stacked two high and four deep – veg, meat, soup, fish. And there was an entire flat pallet of soup in the garage. No shit. Ten by ten, only a few missing from the top corner. A little under one hundred tins of cream of mushroom soup. Must have been a Costco special. Unreal.

Add to that the Pot Noodles, super noodles, pasta, and our own collection of same, plus tins (mainly tuna and soup for us, though a bit more variety, thank God – I can't stand mushrooms, to be honest), and I think we're set. I don't know why I'm telling you all this – you'll have found our bodies, our remains, you'll see how we ate and lived our last days. I guess this is for me, really, an inventory. Dumb. Battery time is running low – down around 15%, only one backup. If I need a list, I should just use a pencil, like the Russians did in space.

Water is, as predicted, the problem. We had a pallet of sports-type 500ml water bottles, testament to Luke's running habit, but it was half empty when this all began. We're down to two. Next door was a bust – one 5 litre bottle by the back door, only about a third full.

I refilled a couple of the smaller bottles from the upstairs cistern, which should be fine, it's all treated water. Still, the thought of drinking it makes me sick. Can't help it. Always been squeamish. I mean, worrying about germs, fucking stupid. And yet.

Even the two house cisterns and the next door ones won't be enough. I thought about trying the neighbour's houses, but I remember seeing people lock up as they left. The power cut should take care of any burglar alarms, but I've heard big vehicles moving periodically on the main road at the back of the house. Getting shot as a looter doesn't seem like an especially bright move.

I don't know what to do.

We could boil rainwater, but it's not raining, and anything that does come out of the sky is going to be carrying poison no treatment will remove – stuff that'll make us even sicker, even quicker. I find myself wondering if I could attack the boiler somehow, get the water out from the central heating pipes, but I've never known anything about all that shit – never had to. Luke knew, and before Luke I rented, and it just never came up.

There's a lake not too far away. We could drive down there with as many bottles as possible, fill them up, bring it all back, boil it... but with that shitty single ring gas stove we'd be boiling all day. Pete had two spare canisters in his garage, bless him, but I doubt they'd last long in constant use.

I feel like crying, thinking about us spending our last couple of weeks eating cold food from cans, while our bodies grow weak and fall apart. It's a horrible image, but I can't seem to shake it, it grows and grows in my mind. I start feeling sick again, not the simple nausea, something deeper, something in the bones. Or worse, the thirst just taking us away. I flash back to my early days in the office, on the phones, the thirty, forty call days, how my throat would start to click from a lack of moisture when I tried to swallow, get painful. I try and imagine that feeling just getting worse and worse, Charley going through it, what have I done to us? Sure, we'd have died just as dead with the soldiers, but at least we wouldn't have died thirsty. The more I try and think about other things, the more my mind is pulled back to those horrible busy days, counting off the seconds until my 11am break, when I could hit the water-cooler and...

Fuck.

FUCK!

The fucking water coolers!

17

Today was tough.

I took my first pill this morning, but of course the effect is delayed, and I won't really start to feel like myself again until at least tomorrow. I've been fatigued, dizzy, not sleeping well. Charley is already bouncing back. She ate a big breakfast – more bread, some dry cereal (the milk in the fridge had already turned), an apple. Just for breakfast.

She's bored.

It's just crap, that's all. Her normal morning routine on a non-school day (and school is most definitely out, let's face it) would involve at least an hour of blobbing in front of Netflix before breakfast.

I explained to her the telly wasn't working any more, same as the lights. I think her being sick, she hadn't really engaged with it properly, and now she's on the mend, she's really noticing how things aren't working. She has a million questions that I can't answer properly.

I managed to distract her with board games, puzzles. I dragged out boxes that we hadn't been in since her birthday, played Frozen and Cinderella and Tooth Fairy over and over. She's basically happy as long as every single moment she has my total undivided fucking attention, and she's doing exactly what she wants. The iPad was fully charged, thank fuck, but I'm making her take her time playing on it – no more than an hour a day. I've tried to explain to her that it won't recharge. She says she understands, but I'm not sure she does.

I'm not sure I do, to be honest.

I tried to keep an ear out through the broken glass, wondering about the evacuation, if there was any more movement. We're not that far from my office, less than a mile. It's five minutes in the car. I just didn't want to get caught by a patrol or another evacuation.

I heard nothing.

Around midday, I told Charley we'd be going out in the car.

"To get Daddy Luke?"

It really felt like the ground lurched under me for a second, like the earth was a seesaw that had just tilted. I felt my breathing get heavier.

"No, lovely. We're going to Daddy Rob's work."

"Why?"

"To get some water."

"Why?"

"Because we need more and there's lots of big bottles of water at Daddy Rob's work."

"Why?"

"Because it's a call centre and when people talk on the phones a lot, they get thirsty."

"Why?"

"Because..."

I felt my voice starting to get louder. Forced myself to calm down.

"Because when you talk a lot you get thirsty."

"Why?"

"Because when you talk, your mouth is open a lot, and that makes the saliva in your mouth dry out."

"Why?"

"Well..." I stopped, then cocked my head, a mock frown on my face. "Wait, are you playing the Why game with me?"

Her laugh was long and loud. Too loud. It hurt my head. I smiled back anyway.

18

I reset the car before we left – put her car seat in the front passenger, pushed the rear seats down flat. I didn't want to make this trip more than once, and I figured with the seats down, I could get eight or ten of the 19 litre bottles in the back, which should be plenty. I eased out onto the main road, willing the car engine to be quieter. It was deserted. Every end of the world movie had taught me to expect abandoned cars all over the place. This was neat. Clean. Like the people had just upped sticks and left.

Which I guess is pretty much what had happened.

The silence and the sunlight and the birds conspired to make my head ache, somehow. At least Charley was quiet, which was a blessing.

We made it to the office without incident, and I pulled up as close to the building as I could. I looked at Charley. She smiled at me. My reply smile felt painful.

"Can I come in, Daddy Rob?"

I stared at her while I tried to decide. I wanted to be quick, that was the thing. In and out. If I could find a trolley, maybe I could get it done in one trip, two max. Otherwise, I was looking at lugging the bottles one at a time – I could probably manage two at a pinch, but this seemed like a spectacularly bad time to invite back trouble. But however quick or slow, you could double it if Charley was with me, asking questions, running around the empty office, getting bored, playing with god knows what...

My head was really starting to throb now, the pain sat behind my left eye like a nail.

"Charley, I don't think that's a good idea..."

"But Daddy Rob, I WANT to COME!"

"You listen! Do not shout at me! Daddy Rob is not feeling well, and I don't need you shouting!"

"But you're shouting at ME!" her voice petulant as well as angry, building to the waterworks. I felt my own anger surging up in response, fuelled by the pain.

"You listen to me, child! You will stay in that chair until I come back, okay? You will sit there and you do not move! Understand? I will be as quick as I can, but you need to sit still. Do you understand?"

"But Daddy Rob..."

"NO! DO YOU UNDERSTAND?"

"It's not fair!" She did start to cry then, great howls of outrage. I climbed out of the car and slammed the door hard enough to make the car rock on its wheels, and through the glass I heard her howling take on a louder tone. I pressed the locking button and stalked towards the office without looking back.

19

I used my master key to get into the building, grateful that the firm had been too cheap to move to the electronic swipe card system that kept being threatened. The building was just two floors, with the back office admin on the ground floor and the actual call centre on the first. Unfortunately, that same cheapness meant that the water coolers were *also* only on the first floor – for the ground floor back office staff, the tap water and refrigerator was deemed sufficient for their needs. Out of habit, I pressed the lift call button, and actually waited for twenty seconds before remembering. Force of habit. I am such a fuckwit.

I checked under the stairs for the trolley, but it wasn't there. The caretaking for the complex was outsourced, and sometimes the firm would leave the moving equipment there.

But not this time. Ah well, would have been a sod to haul up and down the steps anyway.

I made my way up the stairs, trying to ignore how the sunlight through the glass had warmed the air, adding a layer of sweat to my discomfort. I unlocked the top floor door, and then wedged it open – my inner fire warden protested, but I told him to go fuck himself. The office was eerie – a huge open plan empty space, normally full of the drone of conversation, voices overlapping into an incoherent babble that could be desperately distracting or oddly soothing, depending on my mood. Certainly its absence was completely jarring, and I stood still, soaking up the silence, trying to make sense of it, make peace with it.

I'd been here when it was empty before, of course. Perils of management, some days you end up either late or early. But this was different. Those times, crunching numbers or juggling rotas, the place had felt still alive somehow, slumbering, like seeing your parents in pyjamas – the familiar presented in an unfamiliar way. But this... the room yawned. It felt like a cavern.

Abandoned. Like the town.

Like us.

I felt my heart start to race then, panic threatening. I looked down the row of name plates on the desks at this end – the end nearest me, where the permanent staff sat, separate from the temps who occupied the desks nearest the door, last in, first out and all that – John, Marie, Maisy, Paula, Debbie, Roger, Freddie, on and on, faces floating up at me, and I realised with a start that some of them I was already starting to struggle to see, in my mind, people I'd worked with for years. Already fading. It seemed like the room was getting dimmer. Like the sun was passing behind a cloud. I thought I saw

Shit, that's one battery down. Sorry.

Must type faster.

Anyway, I remembered how much Freddie liked his snacks, and I opened up his cupboard, feeling no guilt at all. Inside was a carrier bag containing two multipacks of crisps and no less than four packs of chocolate bars, only one of which was open. There was also a six pack of Coke in the bottom.

I grabbed the carrier bag and put the handles over my wrist. Then I went over to the first water cooler. There were two empty bottles and three full ones. I took the full one from the bottom rack and picked it up, bending at the knees as I had learned on my half day manual handling course. The bottle was heavy, no question, but not painfully so. I got it out to the stairs on one go, and put it down at the top for a second before carrying on. I thought about just rolling it down, but I wasn't confident that either the bottle or the seal wouldn't break, and the fact that half of the bottles had been empty meant that was a risk I really couldn't afford to take. There were three coolers on the floor, meaning if the usage was consistent, there may only be eight or even six bottles. I should have checked, but I didn't, and it didn't even occur to me to go back in and look.

The heat in the staircase had become stifling – or maybe it was just the added effort of lugging the water down – and I had to stop at the landing to get my breath back. I looked out of the window at our car, parked there, and realised I had basically no idea how long I'd been in the building. I thought about Charley in the car seat, and started to feel nervous. She'd be fine, it hadn't been long, it wasn't that hot.

Still.

I ran back up the stairs, opening the fridge in the kitchen area. Sure enough, Freddie had left another six pack of Coke in there, half of them missing. I grabbed one of the remaining cans with a smile, remembering what Luke had told me about bargaining – 'The trick is to give her as a deal something you were going to give her anyway'. I'd seen it work like a charm in the past. I felt a lot of things in that moment, too much to unpick, so I shoved it all down, pushed the can into the bag, and headed back down the stairs to the water bottle.

I didn't bother stopping at the bottom of the stairs, but pushed on through the propped open door. I glanced up at the car, but the light was shining on the windows and I couldn't see in. Couldn't hear screaming either, so I figured she'd calmed down. I moved faster anyway, head down on the bottle I was carrying. One foot in front of the other. Visualizing making this trip six or eight more times. Thinking it wouldn't be too bad, probably.

"That looks heavy."

20

I dropped the bottle, arms suddenly numb, nerveless. It hit the tarmac with a crack.

The man was standing next to my car, arms folded. He had the kind of beard that Luke would sometimes call George Michael stubble. He was older than me. Taller. His size wasn't all muscle, but it wasn't all fat either. He was wearing a tan jacket over a plain black T-shirt. Black jeans and combat boots completed the look. His hair was dark, curly, and short; his eyes pale blue, intense, and gave nothing away.

"I work here. I have keys."

I could feel myself turning red, the heat and panic conspiring. My cheeks burned.

"Is that so?" His voice still calm. No uniform. He wasn't a soldier, wasn't a policeman. But something about how he carried himself...

"Yeah. I didn't break in. I just need the water."

I glanced over his shoulder, through the car window. Charley was slumped in the seat, her eyes shut. I could see the sweat on her brow from here. My stomach lurched and I wondered if I was going to puke.

"What's in the bag?"

I started, looked back at him. His voice was still calm, face deadpan.

"Just some chocolate." The silence hung tight. I felt like I was being pulled, stretched. "You want some?"

"That's very kind, thanks."

I reached into the bag, pulled out one of the bars. I held it out to him, and I could feel the heat in my cheeks, sweat on my brow. He looked back at me, one eyebrow raised. I looked back, unease dipping into something stronger. I flexed my fingers, causing the bar to flap up and down in my hand. He nodded, and I threw the bar over to him. It was a bad throw, but he caught it to his stomach, eyes never once leaving mine.

"Thanks," he said again, putting the chocolate in his jacket pocket.

"Is there more in there?" He gestured at the bottle between my feet. Still calm, still giving nothing away. I found his lack of nerves utterly unnerving. He couldn't have seen Charley. I was frantic to get to get to her, but some powerful urge stopped me.

I didn't want this man to know about her. That was the beginning and end of it.

"Yes."

He nodded once. Face still unchanged.

"How much?"

"Not sure. More than I'll need, for sure."

Was that true? Did it matter?

He stared at me then, let the silence stretch out. I remember Luke telling me about this – basic interrogation technique, say nothing, let the suspect fill the void with more words – but of course, I had a very pressing need to get the conversation finished.

"I'd be happy to split them with you, if you've got use of them."

He nodded some more. "That'd be good, yes. Thanks very much." The politeness, coupled with the controlled neutrality, made my gut churn again. Who was he? What did he know? Why was he here?

"My car is around the front of the building. I'll need to go and get it. This your one?" He gestured at my car.

"Yes."

"Good. Back in a sec."

He turned and started walking away. I looked down at the bottle at my feet, and registered for the first time that it was undamaged. I felt a spike of gratitude then that made me almost dizzy.

"By the way, you might want to give your child a drink. She looks a bit too warm to me." His voice floated over his shoulder, the same plain inflection as before. I stopped reaching for the bottle and grabbed at the passenger side door instead.

21

Charley was groggy, did not want to be woken. I shook her, and eventually her eyes focused on my face. "Daddy Rob, I have a headache."

The way she formed the words, so calmly, without anger, only sadness, made my heart lurch.

"I'm sorry, sweet pea. I'll give you some medicine as soon as we get home."

"Are we going home, Daddy Rob?"

I felt a powerful urge to say yes – to say fuck it, load in the one bottle and just get the fuck home. The guy would probably come back before we'd pulled away, but if I'd read him even close to right, he wouldn't be bothered – might even be happy, able to explore the open office at his leisure, take whatever he wanted. But I pictured the one bottle in my mind, looking at Charley, sweaty, thirsty. No. I couldn't.

It wasn't enough.

"Soon. Look!" I pointed to the water bottle. "Daddy Rob needs to get some more of these, okay? So we have enough to drink at home."

"Are you taking them? From work?"

"Charley, it's okay, work is closed, like school, and they don't need them anymore." I looked at her, pleading for her to understand.

"So it's not stealing?"

I heard a car start up.

"No! No, it's fine, they said we could take them, because it's closed and we don't have any water at home."

"So... they're sharing? With us?"

"Yes, Charley, they're sharing."

"They must be very kindly."

"They are. Listen Charley, I'm going to have to go back in..."

"Can I come?"

"No! No, but..."

"But, Daddy Rob..."

"BUT! IF you promise to stay in the car, like a good girl, you can have this!" I pulled the can of Coke out of the bag.

She looked at me and wrinkled her nose. "Coke?"

"Yes."

"But, you said I wouldn't like Coke. You said it was just for grownups."

I felt tears come to my eyes then. I feel them again now, as I sit here typing, out in the hall so the click of the keys won't wake her. My little girl. Six years old and never tasted Coke. Oh, we thought we were being so good, didn't we Luke? So fucking righteous. Childhood obesity epidemic, diabetes epidemic, well not our little girl, oh no, she's gonna be raised right, none of that fatty shit or sugary shit for her, no Happy Meals, no bags of crisps, and absolutely none of the twin Satans of sugar and caffeine, Coke.

Well, we've cracked it. She'll never eat a happy meal.

Fuck. I'm so fucking sad.

Anyway.

"Well, I think you're a very special little girl, and I think you might be old enough to like it now."

"Really?"

Her eyes lit up. Nothing she likes more than feeling grown up.

"Well, maybe. Would you like to try it? You don't have to."

Her face went very solemn, a small crease appearing on her brow.

"I will try it, Daddy Rob."

I could hear the sound of loose gravel crunching under tires, a sound that always made me think of the playground after school dinners. I glanced up. A white van with a side sliding door was driving towards us. I felt sweat pop on my forehead, and found myself frantically hoping that the vehicle didn't have any more occupants than the driver. I looked back to Charley and tried to smile.

"Okay."

I popped the can and handed it to her. Behind me, I could hear the van slowing down, then stopping. I didn't look around. Didn't want to. Nothing to be done. Let me have this moment.

"Drink like from a bottle, okay? Careful, it's got bubbles."

She held my eyes, nodding, only looking to the can when she was sure I'd finished talking. She carefully brought the can to her lips, slowly tipping it up.

Behind me, I heard the driver door open. Footsteps on gravel.

The liquid finally passed her lips. She tipped the can back quickly. A brown droplet of liquid splashed into the ring tab, sparkling in the sun like a muddy gem.

Her eyes flashed, then her face became solemn again as she turned to me.

"Daddy, I like it!"

Her smile – not grin, no teeth – like she'd passed an important test, crossed some Rubicon, actually made me feel faint for a second.

Then I heard the side door of the van open, footsteps coming towards me. I closed my eyes, took a deep breath, and turned around.

The man was stood a few feet away, in front of his vehicle. I looked past him, verified the interior was empty, let out a breath I didn't know I was holding, then looked back at him. His face held that same neutral expression.

"You ready?"

22

He came with me, back into the office, and we inventoried the bottles. The situation was better than I'd thought – the middle rack also had three bottles, but the one at the far end was fully loaded, with all five bottles full. As soon as I saw it, I remembered how we were in an off peak period, how we'd gotten rid of all the temps that normally sat near the door last month. No-one was using the cooler.

"I make that eleven bottles total."

I nodded, pissed that he'd remembered the one already in my boot.

"Do you think you can fit six in that car?"

The question surprised me. I'd already mentally written off the extra bottle, was wondering if I'd end up begging for what was left, but when I looked over at him I saw no trace of sarcasm or malice – just that same calm, neutral expression.

"Yes, I think so. If you're sure."

He shrugged, not really looking at me.

"Sure. There's two of you."

I did a quick calculation. Six nineteen litre bottles – ninety four litres, so at two litres a day each...

"Should be three weeks' worth there, if you pace yourselves."

I could feel the astonishment on my face, but couldn't change it. His eyes finally met mine, held me.

"Should be enough."

He *knew*. And if he knew, he also knew that half was enough – more than enough – for him, too. I nodded, and he nodded back, and I felt the enormous tension I'd been holding in start to dissipate. It was going to be okay. *He* was going to be okay.

"Okay, let's get these downstairs."

23

The five trips took just under an hour by the dashboard clock in the car. Felt a lot longer, and my arm and shoulder muscles were making their displeasure known. The man had also started sweating, which made me feel better still about him. The can of Coke had kept Charley quiet for a while, and when she started kicking off again as I loaded bottle number four, I gave her one of Freddie's chocolate bars, which chilled her out. Better yet, she expressed a need to pee as the last bottle was loaded, so I had an excuse to linger, let the man drive off ahead. I was pretty sure he was okay and wasn't going to follow us... but 'pretty sure' feels a long way from certain when you have a six-year-old and a house you can't secure.

We shook hands before he drove off. His hand was hot and sweaty, grip firm. "You're Rob, right?" He'd heard Charley call me it.

"Yes."

"I'm Jim."

"Okay." We stopped shaking hands. Looked at each other. "Well, good luck, Jim."

The corner of his mouth twitched.

"Good luck, Rob."

He got into his van, and I heard it pulling away behind me as I took Charley in to use the facilities. By the time we came back out, he was gone.

24

Dug a toilet pit in Pete and Sharon's garden when we got back. I felt bad about it, but they're not going to live to see the mess I've made, and I couldn't face the damage I'd do to either my lawn or the plants. I know it's facile – that first rain will already have irrevocably poisoned the soil for generations, it's all going to rot and die soon enough – but looking over it in the afternoon sunlight, the colours, the leaves, all that growth... I teared up at the thought. Seems like every other fucking thought today made me cry, or want to.

Inventory: ninety-six litres of drinking water (plus four cisterns, here and next door, if things get desperate), chocolate bars, crisps and cans of Coke to add to the food stash. Pete's bulk buying habits also extended to toilet roll, which is handy. I feel like, in the absence of disaster, we're pretty well set to see things out.

Second laptop battery is down to 80%. If I keep writing to this level of detail, it seems likely that this journal will cease long before we do. Maybe that's for the best, too. It's apt to get ugly towards the end. This way, you can remember us at our best.

Tired now. More tomorrow.

25

Christ, I'm shaking. Can barely type.

Today started out so well.

Rice for breakfast, courtesy of Pete and Sharon and their Uncle Ben's boil in the bag goodness. Dietary variety is going to get to be a problem, I think. Right now, it's all still a novelty, and rice for breakfast is a fun adventure. I'm worried about when she starts to feel ill again and starts demanding her cereal, her milk, Marmite on toast.

Shit. Least of my problems, really. It's funny the crap your mind will go to, to distract you from the big stuff. Maybe that's how normal people manage to sleep at night.

Anyway.

After breakfast, Charley asked to go to out on her bike, to the park, and I thought, why not? I'd heard no traffic at all for the last twenty four hours. Seemed to me like there was every chance we had the city to ourselves. Besides, we were both feeling good. She was well, headaches and nausea all gone, and I could feel the second pill levelling me out some – enough that I regretted my paranoia with the stranger the previous day.

The sun was bright, an occasional faint breeze

taking the edge off the heat. I put sunscreen on her before we left, and she was happy enough to be going out that she didn't even protest.

We walked along the edge of the empty road, towards the underpass. The sound of her pedals turning, the tires in the gravel, felt discordant, almost sacrilegious. I tried to tune into her uncomplicated joy, at being five years old and out in the sun on her bike, but every time I felt that pleasure rising in my heart, I felt the silence behind her noise crowding in, grinding against my nerves, threatening a headache. It felt suffocating, somehow, and I sweated into my shirt as we walked along.

"Daddy, there's a bird!"

I looked up. She'd pulled to a halt a few feet ahead, was staring at the path. I jog-walked the few steps to her side, and looked where she was pointing. It was a robin, lying in the middle of the path on its side, the body perfect and unbroken, but rigid. I felt my stomach lurch.

The silence. Total silence. No insects. No birdsong.

"What's wrong with it, Daddy Rob?"

"I don't know, sweetheart. Maybe it's sleeping." I could hear my voice thickening with emotion, couldn't stop it, the enormity of what was happening crowding in, along with that bastard blank silence.

"But it's not breathing. I think it's dead."

I swallowed hard, choking down a sob. When I spoke, my voice sounded rough, but clear.

"Yes, you're right. It is dead."

We looked at the corpse in silence. The sun shone on.

"Do you want me to move it, lovely?"

"No, Daddy Rob, that's okay." She shrugged, and then peddled off, carefully steering around the body.

We passed four more bird corpses on the short journey to the park, the last a huge crow with its left wing splayed out, as if about to take flight. Charley barely glanced at it on her way past. The novelty had already worn off.

This was the new normal.

We made it to the park, and she set off, first to the climbing frame and slide combination, scrambling up the toddler climbing wall, then over to the huge balance beam that ran along one edge of the park, zigging and zagging. I walked over to her, but she refused help, arms out, and I walked back to the bench, and just sat and watched her for a while, eyes squinted against the light.

My little girl. My princess. So brave. So *fearless.* Fierce. Determined. Okay, stubborn. Such physical confidence. No idea where that comes from, I'm a klutz, trip over my own shadow, scared crossing roads, and this kid, oh this kid. As I watched, she completed the whole run, and triumphantly jumped off the end, turning to me with a grin. I clapped.

"Daddy Rob, why are you crying?"

26

We'd moved over to the swings when the old man announced himself. I'd just pushed her and taken a step back when my peripheral vision caught movement. My head snapped around, and I saw a door open in one of the houses facing the park.

He was in his seventies, at least, I think. Thick, black rimmed NHS specs sat on the end of a slightly outsized nose. He shuffled out into the light, moving in that slow and careful way the elderly often develop – especially the ones who live alone, who know there's nobody who will come if they fall.

He was wearing a white shirt, tucked into smart brown trousers. The red slippers were the only incongruity. His eyes met mine, and his gaze was nakedly evaluative. I could see the fear under the surface, and smiled as well as I could manage, raising a hand in greeting.

He didn't smile back, but he nodded, raised his own hand limply in return.

"Lovely day." he offered, blinking in the sunlight as if for effect.

"Beautiful," I agreed, pushing Charley. She glanced over, smiled and waved. The man managed a return smile this time. It made him look older. Sad, too.

He nodded, turning back to me.

"How old is she, your little girl?"

"I'm five years old! I will be six in January."

"Six in January! My word! Growing up fast!"

"Yep!"

"She is that," I said. We held each other's eyes for a moment, then the old man looked down, swallowed. "Yeah, yes, well..." He stared at his slippers, as if seeing them for the first time. Then looked back up at me, this time with a sheepish grin on his face. "So you decided to stay?"

"Yes, well..."

"We're waiting for Daddy Luke!"

He raised an eyebrow, shifted his gaze to Charley. "Is that right? Is he...So, this is your uncle?"

"No, this is Daddy Rob!" She wrinkled her nose. Silly old man. I swallowed, nervous suddenly.

"Right! Right, okay, yes, right. So is, erm, where is 'Daddy Luke', do you think...?" Looking back at me, eyes curious, but I saw no malice, no anger.

"He was at training in London." I said, keeping my voice even, my eyes steady. He nodded once, too quickly, swallowing again,

"Right. I see, yes."

"Daddy! Push!"

"What do we say?"

"Push, please!"

"Good girl." I gave the swing a solid shove, and

she giggled with delight. I looked back at the old man. His eyes seemed suddenly watery, as though the sunlight was getting to them.

"So you decided to stay?"

He looked at me, down to Charley, then back. Nodded. "Yeah. My Elsie passed a few months back..."

"Oh, I'm sorry..."

"...thank you – yeah, and I got diagnosed... erm..." He glanced at Charley again, then me. I shook my head slightly. "...er, well, anyway, I decided I wanted to see things out here. You know?"

"Yeah, I do."

We held each other's gaze. I nodded.

"Yeah. Yes. Well..."

He froze, eyes suddenly on the horizon, looking at the trees that surrounded the park, cutting off the view of the world. I almost asked him what was wrong, then my brain caught up to the sound; a vehicle engine. I reflected on how odd it was; normally, down here, the sound would be constant, background. Now, it sounded alien. Intrusive.

We looked at each other, ears following the sound. It remained constant for a while, then cut out. The vacuum of silence made a mockery of judging distances – it could be nearby, or an estate or two over in any direction. After a while, he shrugged, and we went back to chatting.

We talked a while, Charley content to be pushed and I to push her and shoot the breeze. The engine started up again, and slowly faded. We didn't talk about it, but I saw him visibly relax. Eventually, Charley's hunger got the better of her, and we left. The old man introduced himself as Ralph. We shook hands as we left.

Charley and I made our way home, and I spotted more dead birds on the way back – under trees, laying in the grass. I marvelled again at how perfect they looked. How well preserved, given the heat. It wasn't until later – that evening, as I held my sleeping daughter close to me with one arm, my other underneath my pillow, hand grasping the hilt of the biggest kitchen knife I owned, mind racing, unable to sleep – that it occurred to me why; that I connected the lack of decay with the absence of insects. They'd rot, those bird corpses, no doubt. But without the flies and their young to assist with the process, they'd rot slow.

Anyway.

We chatted as she trundled along, the noise of her bike rattling through the still day like the last machine on earth. We talked about what to eat for tea, what we might do tomorrow. She didn't ask about Daddy Luke, or about where the people had gone. It was all about the world as it is now, the new normal of no school and rice for breakfast and park and games all day and no TV and no baths and sleeping in her clothes. The world was over, and she was singing about soup for tea and giggling.

It took me a second. We pulled into the driveway and I looked at our house, then over to Pete and Sharon's, then back at ours. Charley prattled on, singing about a flying unicorn that had made school disappear, and I looked again between the two houses, waiting for the penny to drop, for the sinking feeling in my stomach to reach my brain and tell me what the fuck the problem was.

Eventually, I realised. Both front doors were open.

27

They'd come through the back, of course. The fence sagged in the middle, where they'd vaulted over. Footprints in the flowers, broken stems. The last of the tulips. There was mud on the carpets. They'd been through every room in the house. I ran straight out to the garage, ignoring Charley's questions, fear slamming me in the chest, making it hard to breathe. But the panic was all for nothing. They'd not gotten in there. The water and food were safe.

Just the electronics gone. I guess they'd missed this laptop, tucked under the bed. Or maybe they just didn't like the look of it – it is pretty old.

Opportunistic, but not too bright.

"Daddy Rob, you're not LISTENING to me."

"I'm sorry, sweetheart. Daddy Rob needed to check the garage was safe."

"Why?"

"I thought they might have taken the water."

She screwed her face up, nose wrinkling in confusion. "Why would they take the water, Daddy Rob?"

"No reason, silly Daddy. Nothing to worry about."

"Why did they take the television, Daddy Rob?"

"I think they thought they could sell it."

"Sell it to who?"

"I don't know, darling."

"But there's nobody here! And anyway it wasn't working!"

"I know."

"So why..."

"Charley, I'm really sorry, I don't know, okay?"

I could feel all the good mood from our visit to the park draining out of me. I thought about the vehicle engine we'd heard while talking to Ralph. I felt a surge of anger, then choked it back. Useless. Even if I'd known I'd never have gotten back here in time. I thought again about the man we'd bumped into at the office. His van. Had he followed us?

Useless. Pointless.

My mind ran over the house, how to secure it. Impossible. All the windows blown out, front and back. Even if I stripped the fence for wood, it would take too long to do tonight. And anyway, I don't know how. Luke was good with tools, and what Luke didn't know how to do, we'd pay someone for. No way. No way to get it done.

"Daddy, where is the iPad?"

I looked over at the arm of the sofa, where we'd left it when we left the house. The battery had been down to 20%, and I'd made Charley stop playing on it. Telling her to save it. Reminding her that when it was gone, it was gone – there was no way to get it recharged. She'd argued. In the end I'd distracted her, talking about the bike, the park. Bribing her with a sports cup full of blackcurrant squash – 'pink juice', she calls it – we're going to run out by the end of the week, I expect, but who cares? Anyway, it worked, she went for it, and when we got back, the iPad and its last 20% of charge were all gone, along with the TV, BluRay player and home cinema.

I looked at her. My brave little girl.

I didn't know what to say.

She saw my face. Looked at me carefully. I could see her thinking, processing.

Then she burst into tears.

I pulled her into my arms and she hugged me tight, face pushed into my chest. I felt her tears soaking into my shirt, her hot breath, and I kissed the top of her head and started crying.

28

We moved into the garage that night. I pretended that wasn't what we were doing, of course. I said we were camping out. But I dragged the double mattress down and out and in, and laid it next to the food. I left the rear door open as we settled down, so I'd have light to read by.

It's funny, but a few days without CBeebies and she's completely converted into a bibliophile. We've got through *Charlie and the Chocolate Factory* and most of *The BFG* in the last couple of days. My throat is feeling tight, scratchy, from all the talking, but she's loving it.

She's asleep now. The knife is under the pillow, the back door locked and shut from the inside, the light from this screen throwing the whole room into a blue haze.

Battery around 35%. Don't know what I'm going to do when that's done. Well, not write, I guess. Use candles.

We'll cope.

I hope sleep will come soon. I hope the men don't come back in the night.

I hope tomorrow is better.

29

She wanted to go to school today, she announced over breakfast.

I looked at her over the bowl of rice. Her face open, serious.

"But sweet pea, the school's closed. I told you, remember? The teachers and children are all gone, school closed. You don't have to go."

"I know that, Daddy Rob. But I just mean, well, I want to go, that's all."

"You want to go to school? Even though it's closed?"

"Yes, Daddy Rob."

"You're a crazy cracker, you know that?"

She laughed, delighted.

"No, I just mean... well, it would be fun to go. You could make me a packed lunch and take me and we could go into the classroom and you could pretend to be teacher!"

"I don't think the classrooms will be open, lovely, I think it'll all be locked up."

"Well..." She thought about it, still hooked into the idea, and I could see she really wanted to go, "yeah, but we could play in the playground and maybe have a picnic on the field." She grinned. "I could put on my uniform and everything! Please, Daddy Rob?"

"Sweetheart, I don't..."

"Pleeeeeeeese?"

I was feeling okay. Even with the scares of yesterday, I was feeling steady. I'd taken my last pill that morning, and knew I had two or three more days of feeling this good, this stable.

Fuck it, I thought.

"Okay lovely. Let's go to school."

"Yeeeeeeeeeessssssssssssss!"

30

The weather was sunny again, the sky clear. The wind blew up from the south. It was borderline hot. She refused her bike and her scooter, and skipped along the path. I glared out at the road beyond the tree line, but it was empty, quiet. The scratching of Charley's shoes on the gravel was the only sound in the world. After a short distance, the constant tugging on my hand became irritating, so I skipped with her. Our held hands swung between us, throwing a shadow onto the path. She laughed. It was like music.

We skipped and walked and skipped some more. I ignored the bundles of feathers at the side of the path, and one pile of fur that was probably a squirrel. Charley didn't notice at all, just bounced along, her green cardigan swinging with her arms.

She slowed as we reached the school. The street was deserted, of course, but it felt even emptier than that. I could see Charley soaking it up – the absence of cars, pedestrians. No gaggle of children, harried parents. No Mr Kent, the caretaker, yelling out greetings from the gate. A street we'd only ever seen as a scene of kinetic, crowded activity, now appeared naked. Skeletal.

I squeezed Charley's hand, and when she looked up at me, I smiled as well as I could. She smiled back, but she didn't resume skipping. I could feel the reality of our surroundings crowding in. It hurt. I let it, but I kept walking.

The main gate was closed, but the side gate was open. I pushed it and we walked through. Charley's face had grown very still.

"Are you okay, pumpkin?"

"Yeah."

"We don't have to go in if you don't want to – if you've changed your mind..."

"No Daddy Rob, it's okay, I still want to go."

"You sure?"

"Yeah. It's just, well, I mean it is quiet, it's quite strange, but I still want to go."

"I know, it's odd, isn't it? Well, it's okay to change your mind at any point, just let me know."

"Okay Daddy Rob, I'm okay."

"Okay."

We'd walked up to the door of her classroom while talking, as much out of habit as anything. It was shut, of course. I lifted Charley up so she could see in the window, over the pictures that were blu tacked up over the bottom of the glass. She pointed out her chair, her drawer, where she hung her coat. The morning sunlight was splashed all over the back wall. We squinted at the finger painting and stick figures outside stick houses, as she tried to remember who had drawn or painted what. She got very excited when she spotted her picture, of Daddy Luke and Daddy Rob holding her hands outside of our house.

"I wish we could take it home with us, Daddy Rob. Hang it on the fridge."

I thought about it. I'd have to break a window, at the very least. Either the orientation of the building or the natural depression the school was situated in had protected the windows from the blast. Or maybe it was safety glass or something. I thought about if I could heave one of the litter bins through the window. The noise, even if it worked.

"I know, baby girl. I'm sorry. We can come back and look at it again... before we leave, if you want." I'd been about to say 'tomorrow' when I caught myself. I flashed back to the iPad. Better to avoid promises I might not be able to keep.

"Okay, Daddy Rob."

I put her down carefully, and we walked hand-in hand across the playground, angling towards the climbing frame.

"Daddy Rob, could we go to the seaside one day?"

"I think that might be a bit difficult, lovely."

"Why?"

"Well, I don't know if we've got enough petrol in the car, for starters. And I don't know how we'd get any more."

"Why?"

I smiled to myself, in spite of the conversational minefield her questions were setting up. I love the Why game, seeing where it'll take us.

"Well, because all the petrol stations are shut."

"Why?"

"Because..."

She'd ground to a halt as we were walking, and I looked back at her. Her face had gone pale, her eyebrows drawn in a frown. I opened my mouth to ask her what was wrong.

"MR. SCRIBBLES!"

She wrenched her hand free of mine and raced across the tarmac towards the grass verge. I took a couple of steps after her before I saw what she was heading towards: a flash of ginger fur, coiled up on the grass.

I ran to catch up with her, worried that she'd touch the corpse, but she didn't. She stopped walking about a foot away, and slowly sank to her knees. I saw her shoulders slump as I came up next to her, and by the time I'd crouched down by her side, arm across her back, she had already closed her eyes, was sobbing. I pulled her to me, but she pushed back, and she opened her eyes and glared.

"Why is Mr. Scribbles dead?"

"I don't know, darling, I don't..."

"WHY IS EVERYTHING ALWAYS DYING?" She

burst into a flurry of tears after this, and I encircled her with my arms, moving to hold her. She was rigid, but didn't push me away again. I held her that way for a while, listening to her cries bounce around the empty playground.

"Daddy Rob, why is Mr Scribbles dead?"

"He got sick, sweetheart. Something in the air made him sick."

"Is it the same as the birds?"

"Yes, lovely, it's the same as the birds."

I waited for the inevitable next question, but it didn't come. Instead, she asked

"Can we go home, Daddy Rob?"

"Of course we can. If that's what you want."

She looked over at the body of Mr. Scribbles. "I don't want to have my picnic here anymore. I don't really want to come to school anymore."

"That's okay, baby girl. You don't have to."

"Good."

We held hands and walked away.

31

We had the picnic in the garden that evening. I'd offered to take her to the park instead, but she only shook her head sadly. We walked back to the house. No more skipping. On the way back she broke down crying again. She said she was sad about the iPad. I gave her a carry cuddle the rest of the way.

She's been down since. Lethargic, slow to smile or laugh. She wanted to go to bed early, and I let her. She seems pale. I mean, she's a pale kid, but... oh, I don't know.

I'm worried that she's getting sick again. It shouldn't be happening, not so soon. We should have at least another three or four days. But she's a kid. Kid physiology. Maybe it all happens faster.

That fucking cat. It's like she's caught something from that cat.

I keep thinking about the questions she asked. The question she didn't ask.

I keep thinking about how I would have answered it.

I don't know.

I don't know.

32

Middle of the night. Rain started coming down, heavy. The noise on the tin roof of the garage is intense. Woke us both up. Charley grumbled. I lit a candle, gave her some juice, read some more to her – *The Faraway Tree*, we're on to now. Eventually she glazed and drifted off. The noise is still hammering, and I can't get back off. Can feel the beginning of a headache coming on. Probably just sleep deprivation. Hopefully.

Laptop battery is down to 18%. Fuck it, need to try and sleep.

33

It rained. All fucking day.

I didn't want her out in it. Luckily, she didn't want to go either. A massive storm came over, but even when it wasn't thunder and lightning, the downpour was relentless, veering between drizzle and heavy drops that pounded the roof and made it hard to hear each other talk. I made a run out to the house and back to grab the stove and tin opener. I cooked with the door open, letting the steam curl out into the grey day. There was still dirt in the rain water. How long had it been? Five days? Six? I thought back to the amazing sunsets we'd been seeing. Thought about how dust motes stirring in sunlight is really dead skin cells, dancing one last pointless spiral. I shuddered.

Even with the door open, the garage got the smell of soup into the walls, where the damp seemed to cause it to cling. Charley, bored, kept asking for things to do – things that she knew we couldn't do: watch telly, go to the seaside (that, again), listen to music, play on the iPad – she had another cry about that – she even asked for a Daddy Luke cuddle at one point, and refused when I offered a Daddy Rob hug instead.

Distraction tactics are hard when there's nothing to do. I did another house dash, and brought back a huge bag of board games and a deck of cards. It killed some time, but she eventually got bored with rolling dice and counting off moves. I tried to teach her Rummy, but she lost patience with the rules. We had enough dice for Yahtzee, but I didn't know where the rules sheets were.

We went to the toilet in a bucket. I left it outside the door, under the lip of the roof. Hopefully it won't fill with water overnight – last thing I need is to be scraping Charley shit off the patio in the morning.

It was painful. The moments ticking away, our last well days, trapped in the fucking garage; the smell, the merciless rain pounding the ground into mud, rapping on the roof, the insistent salesman that won't take no for an answer.

Fucking horrendous. At least she got down early. Bored into an early sleep.

Hopefully, tomorrow will be better. It needs to be. This is going to get hard otherwise.

34

Well, okay, no. That wasn't better.

The worst part about waking up in the garage is the darkness. Once that rear door is shut, it's pitch black. Which helps with the sleeping, of course, but waking up is disorienting. There's this moment where you're between awake and asleep and you don't understand why you can't see – your eyes open to the darkness, feeling like you're blinded, or buried, or trapped in a dream, somehow.

Which was the moment I heard footsteps outside.

I sat up too fast, blood pounding in my ears, making it harder to hear. But I heard it again – shoes moving over gravel, followed by muttered voices. They were low, male, I thought. I couldn't tell if they were talking quietly, or just far enough away that the rain on the roof was disguising what they were saying.

I could feel my heart slugging unpleasantly in my chest – not actually painful, but hard, heavy.

I froze in place, not really thinking of anything that I can recall, just waiting for more sounds, hoping to hear the footsteps move away.

They didn't. The conversation finished and the steps started up again.

Coming this way.

I reached out to the floor by the side of the bed, scraping the concrete with my fingertips, searching for the lighter. It took me a few seconds, and I could feel the tension of the moment threatening to spill over into panic, but then my fingers touched the plastic tube and the feeling receded. I spun the wheel with my thumb and the flame sprung into life immediately, making me wince with its sudden brightness. I touched it to the candle wick, and let the orange glow settle over the room. The footsteps were heading across the drive, I thought – going towards the house, or the garage?

I reached under the pillow and took out the knife.

I crept over towards the front door of the garage, taking the candle with me, holding it by the saucer I'd stuck it into the night before. The footsteps still appeared to be coming, though the fact that there were two or three people made it hard to be sure. The rain was pattering against the metal door, driven by the wind, which didn't help. Having reached the door, I pressed my ear to it, hoping I'd be able to make better sense of what was going on, perhaps even catch some conversation.

There were a couple more steps, still moving closer. Then, an explosion.

Someone had struck the other side of the door a heavy blow. The noise really was like a blast in the small space. I yelled out in shock and pain, my ear drum howling in protest. At the same time, I dropped the candle. The flame stayed lit, for a wonder, but the saucer shattered, spreading wicked slivers of white porcelain across the stone floor.

From outside, I heard male voices, swearing.

I bent, picked up the candle and turned back to the room. Sure enough, Charley was standing up on the mattress, hair adorably matted, face scrunched up, eyes puffy – still half asleep. I pulled on a smile that felt painful and put the hand holding the knife to my lips.

Shhh.

She scratched her head, frowning, but nodded.

"Is there somebody in there?"

No! I thought, and felt a laugh bubble up in my throat. I turned it into a grin, turned back to Charley, and made the shushing gesture again, then said "Yes."

"What are you doing in the garage, mate?" The voice was deep, smooth, the tone conversational but firm. I didn't like it. I tightened the grip on my knife.

"I live here!"

"What, you live in the garage?"

"Don't take the piss! I live in the house, but the windows are all blown out, so I sleep in here nights. It's my house." It was a real struggle to keep my voice even, but somehow I managed it. I did a quick shoulder check on Charley. She was starting to tiptoe over to me, grinning. I waved her back, pointing at the floor, she frowned, looked, understood, retreated to the bed.

There was a pause. Then "So it's your house, is it?"

"I just said that! Look, we've already been picked over, alright? You can see for yourself, the telly and that have been taken, yeah? You've got the whole city. Leave us in peace, okay?"

"Us?"

I'd heard about how shock can hit you like a real thing – like a bucket of ice water over the head. I'd never really felt it until that moment. *Fuck!*

"You got someone in there with you, mate?"

Fuck! I heard movement, footsteps moving up the side alley. Towards the garden gate. I felt sweat prickling then, even through the cold.

"My boy's in here. He's sleeping."

I looked back at Charley, already shushing her again, smiling, winking, hoping she'd see it as a game. For a wonder, she grinned back. I felt a flicker of relief.

"You said you got a boyfriend in there?"

"My BOY! My SON!"

"How old is he?"

Suddenly there was a loud crunch, the sound of wood splintering. The garden gate! My head snapped back to the other door. I looked at the keys hanging inside the lock. Had I locked the door last night, before bed? I'd meant to, for sure – that's why the keys were on the inside of the door.

But had I?

I took a step forward, and felt a sudden sharp stabbing pain in my foot. I looked down and saw the splinters of white porcelain, a couple of spots of blood standing out in stark relief. I felt a shout coming, and turned it into a word.

"CHARLEY!" She jumped, the tone of my voice scaring her, a frown on her face.

"Lock the door! Do it now!"

"But Daddy Rob, I don't know..."

Another crashing sound, louder, followed by the sound of wood falling on concrete. Then more steps, moving along the sidewall, towards the rear of the garage. Charley squealed in fright.

"Just turn the key left!"

"But..."

"NOW! PLEASE!"

She nodded, ran across the room to the door. Her hand touched the keys, and she looked back at me, frantic. I turned my hand anticlockwise, and I watched her knuckles whiten as she tightened her grip on the keys and turned.

"Daddy Rob, it's not turning!"

"Try harder!"

"Daddy Rob, it's NOT..."

The door handle went down, and I heard the frame creak. Charley yelped and ran back from the door. Her feet collided with the edge of the mattress and she fell onto it. I looked up at the door. The handle went down again, and this time I heard a grunt of effort from the other side accompanied by another creak, but the door held firm.

"It's locked!"

"That's right!" I yelled. I heard the dry click in my throat, and hoped it didn't carry. "It's locked!"

"Do you think you could break it down?"

"Just leave! Please! I am armed and I have a child in here! Pick literally any other house in this estate! We have nothing of value!"

"GO AWAY!" Charley yelled, her face red with anger. I held my breath, suddenly afraid to speak. We locked eyes, and I gently waved my arm at her in a calming gesture. She scowled back, but appeared to lose some of her temper.

I heard footsteps move away from the rear door, back down the side of the house, then joined by another set. They moved far enough away that the rattling of the rain on the door began to assert itself again, and I heard murmured conversation.

"Daddy Rob, what's happening?"

I shook my head. My foot was starting to throb, and as I looked down, I saw blood dripping onto the floor. I tried to push the pain back, to hear past the incessant noise of the rain, to pick out words from the muttering, but I just couldn't. Too far away. Too quiet.

I looked back over at Charley. She was staring at me, her face very serious, fully awake now. She opened her mouth to talk, then closed it again. Good girl.

The conversation stopped, and the footsteps moved away, until their rhythm was absorbed by the sound of the rain.

35

We huddled together for hours, as the candle slowly burned down. Charley had passed me the broom from the corner, and I'd swept clear a path to the bed. I'd hopped over to the mattress and sat down hard, injured foot held out in front of me.

"Daddy Rob, you're bleeding."

"I know, darling. Don't look."

"Why not?"

"Because I need to look at it, see how bad it is."

"It's okay, Daddy Rob. I've seen blood before."

"I know you have, sweet pea..."

"When I fell off my bike, there was a LOT of blood, all over my knee..."

"I remember..."

"...So it's okay, I'm not scared. I mean, I am five now, you know!"

"Okay, lovely. Okay."

It was pretty bad – there was a wicked sliver of porcelain sticking out just above my heel, a pool of blood around where it had pierced the skin, already starting to clot. No way to tell how deep it was in, but I'd have to take it out to get a plaster on.

Which was in the house, of course.

Still, one thing at a time.

"I'm going to have to pull it out, Charley."

"No, don't!"

"I've got to, I..."

"NO! You said if I got anything stuck in me not to take it out! You said..."

"...Charley..."

"YOU SAID not to EVER pull it out! You said..."

"I said get a grown up! I'm a grown up! Okay?"

"But Daddy Rob..."

"No, Charley. It's okay, little girl. You don't have to look if you don't want to, but I've got to take it out..."

"NO! Daddy Rob..." tears in her eyes now.

"Charley, it's okay, honestly..."

"Please, Daddy Rob! Please be careful!"

I looked her in the eyes. Rubbed her cheek, her chin. "Charley, I promise, I know it looks scary, but I promise it's going to be okay, all right? Charley?"

She blinked, and two tears spilled down her face.

"I just want you to be okay, Daddy Rob."

I pulled her face into my chest and stroked her hair. "I'm going to be okay, princess. I'm going to be okay. Okay?"

"Okay, Daddy Rob."

"Okay."

I pulled the splinter out. It hurt. About a half inch had pushed into the soft flesh of my foot, and it left a hole that stung and bled profusely. I used one sock folded up to block up the hole, and tied it on with the other. It wasn't too sanitary, but it would at least stop the bleeding until I got into the house and to the first aid kit in the upstairs bathroom.

Only I couldn't leave.

I tried. I approached the door twice, put my hand on the key the second time. But I couldn't bring myself to turn it. I kept hearing the door creaking in its frame as the man tried to force it. The rain just fell and fell, rattling against the roof, and I kept imagining I could hear shuffling feet, right on the edge of hearing, like someone was out there, in the rain, holding watch. I looked back at Charley, and felt my fear leap to her.

"Daddy Rob, don't open the door."

"I need to get to the house, little one. I need to get a plaster."

"No, Daddy Rob. Don't open the door. Stay with me. Play a game with me. I'm hungry."

I could feel her reaching, pleading, for the thing that would make me stay.

So I stayed.

We ate rice, and played the Cinderella slipper game. Then we played The Three Pigs game. Then we played Going To The Shops. Outside the rain just fell and fell and fell.

36

It was the need to piss that did it, eventually.

"Little girl, I have to open the door to get the bucket, okay?"

"No! Daddy Rob..."

"Can you hold it?"

She squirmed, grimaced.

"Exactly."

"But Daddy Rob..."

"I have to! Okay? I'm busting too. Okay? I have to. I'll be quick. Okay? I promise, I'll be quick."

She frowned, clearly upset.

"Please be fast, Daddy Rob."

"I will be."

I touched the key. Felt the cold metal against my skin. Felt the sick throbbing in my foot. I took a deep breath, and slowly turned the key.

It didn't turn.

I tried again, but it still didn't move.

I tried the handle. The door swung open.

It was unlocked.

It had always been unlocked. He must have pushed instead of pulling.

Everything started to feel very far awa

<audio transcript begins>
Date stamp: xx/xx/xx xx:xx:xx

MALE (MUTED): Test. Test. Test. Do we have lift off?

<ends>

—

<audio transcript begins>
Date stamp: xx/xx/xx xx:xx:xx

MALE (MUTED): So this is working. That's good. That's good. Sorry for the whispering. Charley is asleep. Don't want to wake her.

I've…I mean, I will try to remember to leave this with the laptop. The laptop has a file on it, called 'journal'. I saved it on the desktop. The battery died, but the laptop is working. So, you know, charge that up before listening to this. Because, spoilers.

<laugh>

So if you've read that… Okay, it's been two days since the men came. And we've basically not been out of the garage. I feel safer in here. Not safe, you understand. Just safer. I lock the door all the time now.

It finally stopped raining yesterday. I tried to talk Charley into coming out into the garden, but she wasn't having it. She's not looking well again. Pale, bags under her eyes. She's not sleeping well. Nightmares. Keeps waking me up, so I'm not sleeping well either.

Jesus, I'm tired. And my foot is killing me.

It's not good in here. The air feels stale. Everything smells of boiled rice and soup. The pitch black and the silence. Only the sound of her breathing. Right now, there's a red glow coming from the record light on this dictaphone. It looks like everything is bleeding.

There's a tiny whine coming from the recorder. Don't know why. Guess it's a mini hard drive or something. I don't understand gadgets, that was... uh, that was Luke's thing.

<sigh>

Luke got me this. I'd told him I was thinking about doing some writing, maybe. I'd told him. Said I had this idea for a story, where the person was dictating it. So he bought me this, out of the blue. He is... Sorry. Sorry.

<sigh>

He was sweet like that. A good man. My good man. A good father, too. Once Charley came along, that was the writing done. Never stood a chance, really. Though I'd kept putting it off, too. He must have known that about me. But he bought it anyway.

<sob, sigh>

I miss you so much, Luke. Your little girl misses you. She keeps going on about the cat, and the men. Jesus, a million questions about the fucking men. But it's really all you, babe. You're what she's missing. I can't tell how much she's figured out. I can't tell if she...

<sound of movement>

MALE (WHISPERED): I don't know if she knows she's dying. That we're dying. That you're already dead. She's a bright kid. So bright. I can't tell if all this anxiety is her fronting for that understanding, or if it's just what it is. I don't know if I should tell her. I don't know anything. I don't want to lie to her. I don't want to scare her. She's going to start getting sick again soon. If she hasn't already. Can't tell where stress and bad diet and no exercise and bad sleep ends and the sickness begins.

I wish we could get back into the house. I wish I'd never moved the mattress out. I wish it hadn't rained that day before the men came.

I don't know what to do, now. That's the bottom of it. I can feel myself getting more and more wound up. My back is aching from the mattress on the floor. My throat is sore from all the talking, the reading. My foot is throbbing constantly, really tender. Can't put any weight on it. And I'm out of my fucking pills.

But, yeah, I don't know.

I don't want to deny her anything. What's the point, at this stage? I just want her to be happy.

But she isn't. Not stuck in this fucking garage.

I don't know what to do.

Fuck it.

<ends>

<audio transcript begins>
Date stamp: xx/xx/xx xx:xx:xx

MALE (MUTED): Oh man, I don't know if I can keep this up. I really don't. It feels scary to say that out loud, but...
CHILD: Daddy Rob, why are you talking?
MALE:
Sorry baby girl, did I wake you?
CHILD: I think so. Daddy, I have a sore throat.
MALE: Oh darling. Do you want some medicine?
CHILD: Do you have pink medicine?
MALE: Of course, sweetheart. Hang on a sec...
<ends>

—

<audio transcript begins>
Date stamp: xx/xx/xx xx:xx:xx

MALE (WHISPERED): She's getting sick again. That was the last of the child ibuprofen. Hoping that'll get her through the night. After this, I'll need to get the adult medicine down her, somehow. Which means we have to get out of here, back into the house. I've done all the adult ibuprofen we had out here trying to get my foot under control. Hasn't worked, but at least I've been able to sleep. But I'm out now.

Shit. That'll be fun.

So the headaches started back for her this

morning. Poor kid. She didn't want to get out of bed, complained when I lit the candle. Said the light was hurting her eyes. Then we had a fight about getting the door open. I had to. I mean, I *had* to. Everything in this room feels damp, now. It's horrible. Like being coated in a cold slime. We need fresh air. We need daylight. I talked to her, Reasoned with her. Pleaded. Promised I'd sit by the door the whole time, that I'd listen, and that I'd shut and lock it if anyone came. She wouldn't have it. Started yelling. I had to tell her that if she yelled, it made it more likely someone would come. I had to raise my own. Then she told me off for yelling.

I swear, I came so close to losing it.

I told her that I was going to open the door, and that I'd make her be quiet if I had too. She looked hurt. That's no way to talk to children, she said. I said to be a good girl and I wouldn't have to. She sulked, but I got the door open.

The breeze was a relief. The garden lawn looked inviting, but I noticed the trees were shedding leaves. The silence... it's like being deaf. You don't realise how much you're used to background noise. Traffic, birds, all of it. Now, there's just the breeze through the leaves and branches.

I've got to sort this going out thing. She's okay with me opening up to get the bucket in and out, when one of has to go. I try and go when she does.

The less time the bucket spends in the garage the better. But she won't let me go outside, even to shit. She's terrified of me being out of sight, even for a second.

And I get it. I do. I don't want to leave her, either. It's so stupid. I'd hear anyone coming about a million miles off. But I keep thinking about the men. The ones who took the iPad. The ones who would have gotten in here, if they'd pulled instead of pushed. Jesus, it makes my heart race just to think about it. Daddy Rob, your heart's beeping, she'd say.

Charley girl. What am I going to do with you?

I need to think this through. I need to work this out. I need to work out how to get her out of the garage. Tomorrow. Got to do it tomorrow. It's not going to get any easier. She's getting sick again. Every day she's going to feel less like getting up, getting out. I want her to feel the sun on her face again. I just want...

<sobbing>

<ends>

—

<audio transcript begins>

Date stamp: xx/xx/xx xx:xx:xx

MALE (WHISPERED): Sorry. Sorry. Shit. Got to get it together. Okay, strategies. Luke always said distraction worked when she didn't want to do something. He was so good at that. I'd always just try and make her. Get angry. Do as you're told, kind of thing. Luke, he'd dance through all that. Distract her, then before I knew it, she'd be doing what I wanted with a giggle.

Okay, so there's that. What else? Talk to her. You're scared? So am I. Can you be brave for me? Can you hold my hand? I need to go out because... why? Because my foot is sore. I think the fresh air will help. Yes. Something like that. I'll have to play it by ear a bit. Staying calm is key. Try not to get wound up, angry. So hard, that. So fucking tired now, so sore.

Make a game out of it? That might work, too. Can't see how, but maybe. Yeah.

Oh, man. So tired now. Hope she sleeps through.

<ends>

—

<audio transcript begins>

Date stamp: xx/xx/xx xx:xx:xx

MALE: So, say hello, Charley.

CHILD: *<inaudible>*

MALE: You need to talk a little louder, honey...

CHILD: I don't want to!

MALE: But it'll be fun! Remember what we said?

CHILD: I don't want to, Daddy Rob!

MALE: Okay, okay, look just...

<ends>

<audio transcript begins>
Date stamp: xx/xx/xx xx:xx:xx

MALE: Okay now?
CHILD: Okay, Daddy Rob.
MALE: Good. So why don't you say who you are?
CHILD: My name is Charley Hartwell Anderson, and I am five years old!
MALE: They can't see that, sweetpea, there's no camera. But they can hear you. So, what are we going to do today?
CHILD: We're going to go back into the house.
MALE: And why are we going back into the house?
CHILD: Um, because we need to get some more clothes, and um, some toilet rolls, and also... Oh! We want clean sheets for the bed from the cupboard.
MALE: That's right...
CHILD: ...and Daddy Rob is feeling scared so I am going to hold your hand so you don't have to be scared.
MALE: Thank you, baby girl, that's very kind. Shall we go?
CHILD: Let's just go!
MALE: Let's just go!

<sounds of a door opening, closing, footsteps>

Put your boots on, honey.
CHILD: Why, Daddy Rob?
MALE: Because we're going into the house and

there's broken glass and I don't want you hurting your foot like Daddy Rob did.

CHILD: Why?

MALE: Because then it would hurt like Daddy Rob's foot does.

CHILD: Why?

MALE: Because...

CHILD: *<giggles>*

MALE: Argh! You Why gamed me!

CHILD: I was Why gaming the whole time!

MALE: Clever clogs! Go on, put your wellies on.

CHILD: Why?

MALE: Ha ha. Now please, Charley.

CHILD: But why, Daddy Rob?

MALE: Charley, we can't go into the house unless you put your boots on.

CHILD: Okay, Daddy Rob. No need to shout.

MALE: I'm not shouting. Please just do as you're told.

CHILD: I am doing!

MALE: Thank you!

<shuffling sounds>

Can you hold my hand while we go upstairs?

CHILD: Are you scared, Daddy Rob?

MALE: A little bit, yeah.

CHILD: Don't be scared, Daddy Rob. I'm not.

MALE: Thank you, little one.

CHILD: It's so muddy!

MALE: I know. What do we need, little girl? Can you remember?

CHILD: We need clothes, and pills, and, um… bedsheets!

MALE: Yes! Clever girl, well remembered. Anything else?

CHILD: Erm… maybe some teddies?

MALE: Good idea! Anything else?

CHILD: Umm…

MALE: What about some more books?

CHILD: Yes, Daddy Rob! Can I pick?

MALE: Of course, baby girl, anything you want.

CHILD: Yay!

<footsteps going away>

<ends>

—

<audio transcript begins>

Date stamp: xx/xx/xx xx:xx:xx

MALE: Okay baby girl, we got everything in the bag?

CHILD: Yup!

MALE: Sure?

CHILD: Well, I mean, we can always come back if we forgot anything.

MALE: We can, Charley girl, but I'd rather not. My foot is really sore, and I don't want to do the stairs again if I don't have to.

CHILD: Well, I don't think there's anything.

MALE: Okay, good.

CHILD: Wait, can we take this picture of you and Daddy Luke?

MALE: You want to take this picture?

CHILD: Yeah. I like it. You look so happy.

MALE: Okay, baby girl. Put it in the bag.

CHILD: There we go!

MALE: Okay, all set?

CHILD: All set!

MALE: Awesome job!

<a single hand clap>

CHILD: Let's just go! Daddy Rob, are you okay?

MALE: Fine. Fine. Bag is heavy, that's all.

CHILD: Are you sure?

MALE: Sure I'm sure. Let's go down now. Are you okay to walk behind me?

CHILD: Why?

MALE: In case I drop the bag.

CHILD: Why?

MALE: Charley. It's not a game.

CHILD: But Daddy Rob, I was just...

<crashing noise, child's scream, footsteps>

Daddy Rob! Daddy Rob! Daddy Rob! Daddy Rob, wake up! Wake up, Daddy Rob! Daddy Rob, wake up right now! Daddy Rob. Oh, no!

<sobbing>

Daddy Rob, please, you have to wake up! Daddy Rob, I'm sorry, I'm sorry, please wake up! Oh, this is all my fault! The picture was too heavy, I shouldn't have... Daddy Rob! Daddy Rob.

<kissing sound>

There, a princess kiss. Now you have to wake up. You have to wake up now Daddy Rob. Oh, why won't you wake up? Do you need wet tissue? For where you bumped your head? Will that help? Okay, I will go and get some wet tissue, Daddy Rob, I will come straight back.

<footsteps, receding>

<3 minutes 27 seconds of silence>

<footsteps returning>

Here you go, Daddy Rob, I used the flannel in the bathroom but there was no water in the taps so I had to use the toilet but there was no wee or poo in it so I guess it was okay because you're not drinking it, so, yeah, anyway, I hope...

MALE: *<yelling>*

CHILD (SCREAMING): Daddy Rob!

MALE: ...Leg! Get off...

CHILD: Sorry, Daddy Rob, sorry...

MALE: ...Jesus fucking Christ...

CHILD: ...Daddy Rob, you're awake, you're...

MALE: ...Oh, shit shit shit shit...

CHILD: ...Daddy Rob! Daddy Rob, I love you so much...

MALE: ...Oh, God, Charley I love you too, ah, God that hurts so much...

CHILD: ...Daddy Rob I'm so sorry! I didn't...

MALE: ...Shh, shh, baby girl, not your fault, not your fault, just...

CHILD: No, Daddy Rob, it is my fault, I...

MALE: Charley! Not. Your. Fault. Stop it. Stop.

CHILD: Okay, Daddy Rob. No need to shout.

MALE: Charley, it hurts, okay? It really, really hurts.

CHILD: I'm so sorry, Daddy Rob. I wish I could make it stop.

MALE: I wish you could too, kiddo.

CHILD: Here...

MALE: Careful...

CHILD: ...of course, Daddy Rob.

MALE: That is nice. Thank you, Charley. You're a good girl.

CHILD: I just love you, Daddy Rob, that's all. You are hot.

MALE: It's the pain. Making me sweat. Thank you, that's really cooling me down.

CHILD: That's Okay, Daddy Rob. You take care of me all the time. I can take care of you a little bit!

MALE: You're a good girl, Charley.

CHILD: I know. You're a good Daddy, Daddy Rob.

<40 seconds of elevated breathing>

MALE: Charley?

CHILD: Yes, Daddy Rob?

MALE: I'm really hurt, baby girl.

CHILD: I know, Daddy Rob. I'm so sorry.

MALE: Not your fault, kiddo. Not your fault.

CHILD: What are we going to do now?

MALE: I think… I think I need to sit up, sweet pea. I need to try and get a look at my leg.

CHILD: Can I help?

MALE: Yes. But let me scoot back first, okay? Get to the wall. Then you can help me sit up.

CHILD: Okay, Daddy Rob.

MALE: Good girl. I think this is going to hurt. I'll try not to shout but I might not be able to help it. Don't be scared, okay?

CHILD: Okay, Daddy Rob, Okay, don't worry, I hope it doesn't hurt.

MALE: Me too, kiddo. Okay…

<shuffles, grunts>

MALE: Ah! Okay, okay, okay.

CHILD: Daddy Rob, you're really sweaty.

MALE: I know baby girl, I know. Sorry. It really hurts.

CHILD: Do you need some medicine? I could try…

MALE: No. No, just stay here.

CHILD: But you're hurt, I want to help…

MALE: You are helping. Charley. You are helping. I need you here. Okay? I need you here.

CHILD: Daddy Rob, I want to go home. I mean, not home, we are home, I mean, well, I want to go back to the garage. I don't like it out here.

MALE: I know, baby girl, I know, we're going back, okay? We're going back. Just let me get sat up, okay?

CHILD: Okay, Daddy Rob.

MALE: Good girl. Now, come and stand next to me, okay?

CHILD: Here?

MALE: Perfect. Okay, not greenstick, but definitely broken...

CHILD: Daddy Rob, what's greenstick?

MALE: Nothing baby girl, don't worry.

CHILD: I think that must not be your lucky leg, Daddy Rob.

MALE: ...What?

CHILD: Well, I mean, you cut your foot and now you've factored it...

MALE: ...fractured, lovely. Fractured.

CHILD: ...fractured, I mean, well, it's not very lucky, is it?

MALE: No, I suppose not. Although...

<laughter>

CHILD: What's funny, Daddy Rob? Did I say something funny?

MALE: Yeah. No. Well... at least I still have one good leg to hop on. I guess that makes it a lucky break.

CHILD: Well, at least you're laughing, that's good I guess. Are you laughing, Daddy Rob? Or are you crying?

MALE: Laughing. Laughing, little girl.

CHILD: Promise?

MALE: Promise. Mostly.

CHILD: Mostly?

MALE: Doesn't matter. Okay, little girl. I'm going to need to try and get up now. I'm going to try and slide up the wall, okay? I need to put my hand on your shoulder, all right? I'll try and use it just for balance, but I might have to lean on you a little. I need you to be really, really brave and as strong as you can be, okay?

CHILD: Okay, Daddy Rob. I will be brave. Try and be gentle.

MALE: Thank you, baby girl. I will try. Are you ready?

CHILD: I am ready, Daddy Rob.

MALE: Okay. Here we go. One, Two, Three...

<sliding, grunting, child's cry>

CHILD: Daddy Rob, that hurt!

MALE: Sorry. Sorry. Thank, you baby girl. Thank you, brave one.

CHILD: It's okay, it only hurt a bit, you squeezed me really tight

MALE: I know, I know, I'm sorry.

CHILD: It's okay. I'm glad you're up.

MALE: Me too, kiddo, me too. Okay. Just let me catch my breath for a minute, then we can start heading back.

CHILD: Okay, Daddy Rob. I guess you must be quite tired.

MALE: Do I look tired?

CHILD: Well, I mean, I guess you do. You look like Daddy Luke after he's been running, not sleepy tired, but well, you know. I guess you'd like a rest anyway, yeah.

MALE: A rest sounds good, yes.

CHILD: Well, let's get you back to the bed, okay? Then you can have a lie down if you'd like.

MALE: I'd like that very much, thank you.

CHILD: Okay, fine, can we go now?

MALE: Yep. I'm going to have to hop. Can you walk alongside me, please, for balance?

CHILD: Oh, sure! Just try not to squeeze me again.

MALE: I will try.

CHILD: Thank you, Daddy Rob.

MALE: Thank you, baby girl. Are you ready?

CHILD: Yeh. Let's just go!

MALE: Let's just go!

<shuffling, grunts, receding>

Can you go ahead and open the back door, lovely?

CHILD: Oh, sure! Of course I can.

MALE: Thank you. Brave girl. Helping her daddy.

CHILD: Oh, it's fine, I mean, I like helping, so.

MALE: I know you do, baby girl, I know you do. Okay.

CHILD: Ready?

MALE: Ready.

<shuffling, grunting, inaudble speech>

<seventeen minutes thirty-seven seconds silence>

<footsteps approaching>

CHILD: Where is it? Where did it go? Why...

<fading out>

<fading in>

will be so sad if I can't find it! Oh, think! Here's where he fell over. It can't be far. It's not under here... I wonder if... Yes!

<rustling noise>

I am SO glad I found you! Daddy Rob will be really happy. I know he likes talking to you, I think it makes him feel better. I'm not sure why. Anyway, I'm Charley. Well, you know that, don't you? Yeah, I already said that. Well, I don't know who you are, but hello. My Daddy, well, Daddy Rob, he's one of my Daddies, yeah, anyway, he fell down the stairs and he's broke his leg, so I had to help him go back to the bedroom, well, not the bedroom, but the garage, and then, well, he asked me to come and find this so he could talk some more, he said he had a special story to tell me, but he needed this to tell it for some reason, not really sure why... Anyway, so I think he wants to tell you the story too, for some reason. So, um, I'm going to bring you to him now, okay? Okay.

<footsteps, a door opening, a door closing, more footsteps, a door opening, a door closing>

Daddy Rob, Daddy Rob, look! I found it!

MALE: Good girl, oh, good girl! Come here! You did really well. I'm so proud of you.

CHILD: I wasn't even scared! Well, I was a little bit, but not much.
MALE: Such a brave one, such a brave one. Good girl, good girl. Bring it over here, would you?
CHILD: Oh, sure! Here you go.
MALE: Thanks.
CHILD: Daddy Rob, you don't look well, at all.
MALE: I'm okay, baby girl. I'm okay. Thanks for this.
CHILD: You're welcome, Daddy Rob. Is it story time now?
MALE: Nearly, yes. Can you get me a glass of water please?
CHILD: Oh, yes, of course!
MALE: Thanks, little girl.
CHILD: Oh, that's no problem at all!
MALE: Thank you. So thirsty. Are you thirsty?
CHILD: I'm all right for right now.
MALE: Okay. Help yourself if you want a drink, okay?
CHILD: I will, Daddy Rob.
MALE: Okay, story time.
CHILD: Ooh, goodie!
MALE: Now this is a very special story, about two men called Rob and Luke...
CHILD: ... do they have a little girl called Charley?
MALE: I don't want to spoil the story. Just listen, okay?
CHILD: Okay, Daddy Rob.

MALE: Thank you. Okay. So once upon a time, there was a man called Rob. Robert was his full name, but everyone called him Rob. And he was born and grew up in London.

CHILD: Ooh! Where Big Ben lives?

MALE: That's right, sweetheart. Rob's mummy and daddy were called Rachel and Ron. They… they were good people. They cared about others, and they taught Rob to care about others too. Rob's dad was a bus driver, and his mum worked in an office. They worked hard, and they took care of me… of Rob.

CHILD: Is this story about you, Daddy Rob?

MALE: Yeah. Yes it is. It's my story. Is that okay?

CHILD: Oh, of course! I want to hear it.

MALE: Okay, good. So my mum and dad, your Nanny and Grandad. They were a good mummy and daddy to me. They looked after me, and they taught me to read. Dad was a trade unionist, and…

CHILD: What's a, Daddy Rob, what is a…

MALE: …a trade unionist is… well, okay, you know Daddy Rob works in an office, yes?

CHILD: Yes! Where we got the water!

MALE: That's right.

CHILD: And the Coke and chocolate!

MALE: That's right! In fact… would you like a Coke right now? And a chocolate bar?

CHILD: Really?

MALE: Yes.

CHILD: I can have a whole can?

MALE: If you want. They're in the bag.

CHILD: Okay! Thank you, Daddy Rob. You can keep telling your story while I get them. I mean, I will keep listening.

MALE: All right. So anyway, all I mean is that they were good people, your Nanny and Grandad...

CHILD: Are good people!

MALE: Right. Are.

CHILD: We saw them two months ago, remember? When we went to London on the train.

MALE: I remember.

CHILD: Silly Daddy Rob!

MALE: Silly me. Anyway, yes, they are good people, and they... well, Charley, you remember how Daddy Luke and I told you that sometimes, most times, boys like girls and girls like boys, but sometimes boys like boys and girls like girls, and it doesn't matter either way?

CHILD: Yeh.

MALE: Okay, well, when Daddy Rob was a little boy, he always knew he liked other boys. But when Daddy Rob was little, people weren't always kind about that. Some people... some people thought it was wrong.

CHILD: Wrong? You mean, naughty?

MALE: Yeah. Yes, I suppose. They thought it shouldn't be allowed, or that it... that boys who liked boys were... ill somehow, or broken, or something.

CHILD: Well, that's ridiculous!

MALE: <*laughs*> Well, I know, darling, but that's how it was. It's a lot better now than it was then. Anyway. The point is, Nanny and Grandad were never… they never thought that is was wrong, or a problem, or anything. They were always happy for me to just be happy. They were good parents. Are good parents, sorry. Sorry.

Anyway. School was not easy for me. I was picked on by mean children who didn't like me because of who I was. And also… Okay, Charley, you know about wars?

CHILD: Yes. There were World Wars, weren't there?

MALE: That's right. There were. And you know there were bombs? You know what bombs are?

CHILD: Like in Spelunky?

MALE: Like that, yes, only in real life they were dropped out of planes, onto soldiers, and also sometimes towns and cities. Well, towards the end of World War Two, the scientists built a very special new type of bomb. It was many, many times more powerful than any other bomb we'd had before. It was big enough to blow up a whole city.

CHILD: Wow.

MALE: Yeah.

CHILD: Was it… Did the baddies build it?

MALE: It… no, it was our side. And Charley, we used it. Twice. We blew up two cities.

CHILD: Two baddie cities?

MALE: Well. The cities belonged to the people we were at war with. But they were full of ordinary people, like you and me, who were just trying to live.

CHILD: Why did we do that?

MALE: Because we thought it would end the war.

CHILD: Why?

MALE: Because we thought it would make them so scared that they'd just give up.

CHILD: Why?

MALE: Well, because once they knew we could destroy whole cities, and that we were willing to do it, I think we thought they'd have to give up.

CHILD: *<giggles>* Daddy Rob, I was Why gaming you!

MALE: Wow. Good one. You got me. Anyway, after the war was over, there was a... one of the countries who helped us in the war didn't want to be friends when the war was over. And we didn't want to go to war with them, and they didn't want to go to war with us, because it would be too big and too hard, but we weren't friends. So we, well, our side, the Americans, built lots and lots and lots of these bombs. And the other side, Russia, they built lots and lots of these bombs too. Enough to blow up the whole world, actually.

CHILD: Why? No really, why. I'm not Why gaming you, I want to know.

MALE: Well... the idea was that if everyone had these bombs, everyone would be too scared to use them. Because they knew that the other side had so many that if we attacked them, they'd be able to wipe us out, and the same the other way around.

CHILD: But...

MALE: I know. The thing is, my mum and dad, Nanny and Grandad, they thought it was crazy too. And they kept trying to do things to stop the government from building more bombs, and to try and get them to dismantle the bombs they had built, to make the world safer.

CHILD: Did it work?

MALE: No. Not really, but eventually things changed in Russia and they weren't as angry with us anymore so it got less scary and we all basically stopped building more bombs. But when I was your age, I was very scared about the bombs. I used to go on protest marches, where lots of people who were worried about the bombs would all go together and wave banners, and sing songs and listen to speeches...

CHILD: Like Pride day?

MALE: A bit like that, yes. A bit like that. But the point is, I used to have nightmares about the bombs going off. I knew we lived in London, and I knew we were the capital city and that meant, if there was a war, and the bombs were used, I knew they'd aim them at London. Because it's the capital, where the government lives, and if it was a war, they'd want to try and take out the government.

So I had nightmares, where I'd be woken up by a bright flashing light, and then a loud bang. I'd see a fireball outside the window, and as it reached me, I'd wake up. Sometimes I'd cry out, and Grandpa or Nanny would come.

CHILD: Like when I have belly aches in my foot?

MALE: Yeah. A bit like that.

CHILD: I am sorry you had nightmares when you were a child, Daddy Rob.

MALE: It's okay, baby. But thank you. Anyway. I just wanted you to know about that part of the story. It's not the main bit.

The main bit is, being a boy who liked other boys was easier in London than in a lot of other places, because it's a very big city, so there are more of all different types of people. Including boys who like boys. So there were so many of us we had special clubs we could all go to and be safe. And meet each other.

CHILD: Is that where you met Daddy Luke?

MALE: No. Daddy Rob had other boyfriends before Daddy Luke, pumpkin.

CHILD: Did you?

MALE: Yeah.

CHILD: How many?

MALE: Erm. A few.

CHILD: Really? Did you live with them all?

MALE: No. Not most of them. I lived with Nanny and Grandad for a long time, while I went to University and got my first couple of jobs. But eventually, I did meet one boy I really liked, and we moved in together.

CHILD: Was it Daddy Luke?

MALE: No. No it wasn't. It was a boy called James.

CHILD: Really?

MALE: Really. We met at one of those clubs and I fell in love straight away. He was an amazing dancer. Just perfect. Like a ballerina. Graceful. And he was so handsome. And he really liked me, too. We met and I knew. I knew I wanted to live with him. Share my life with him. I thought he was perfect.

CHILD: But... what about Daddy Luke?

MALE: That was later.

CHILD: But... if you love James...

MALE: I loved him.

CHILD: Then what...?

MALE: *<sigh>* He died, lovely. James died. He got sick and he died. There was... There was an illness. It, um, it... it took people a while to find out about it, and how it got caught, and by the time we knew about it, a lot of people had already caught it, and they got sick and died. James got sick and died.

CHILD: Did you get it, Daddy Rob?

MALE: No. I didn't. I was very, very lucky, but I didn't catch it, from James or... anyone else. But I was very sad, after James died. For a long time. And eventually, I realised I needed to leave London. It was making me sad, being where I'd been with James. The company I worked for opened a new office here, in Milton Keynes, so I moved.

CHILD: And then did you meet Daddy Luke?

MALE: Yes, baby. Then I met Daddy Luke.

CHILD: How did that happen? Was it at a special club?

MALE: No, it wasn't. It was *<laughs>* he came to my house.

CHILD: Huh?

MALE: I know, right? He just turned up on the doorstep one day.

CHILD: But... why?

MALE: Well... I'd been burgled.

CHILD: Burgled?

MALE: Yes. Like when... you know when we were out at the park, and when we got back someone had taken the TV.

CHILD: And the iPad!

MALE: Right, and the iPad...

CHILD: And I never got my last go on it!

MALE: Charley, I know, I'm so sorry about that...

CHILD: ...well, I mean I am quite sad about it, but it's okay, I mean, it's not really your fault.

MALE: How's your Coke?

CHILD: It's delicious!

MALE: Good. Anyway, it was like that. I'd been at work, and I came home and a window had been broken, and a lot of my things were missing. My TV, my computer, things like that. So I phoned the police, and...

CHILD: ...and they sent Daddy Luke!

MALE: They sent Daddy Luke. That's right. And he was very kindly to me, and I really liked him, but I wasn't sure if he liked me...

CHILD: But he did, Daddy Rob! He loves you.

MALE: Yes. Yes, baby girl. He does. Anyway. So Daddy Luke became my boyfriend, and after a while we moved in together, and then later, we had you.

CHILD: Daddy Rob?

MALE: Yes?

CHILD: You always said when I was older, you'd tell me how you had me. I mean, where... I mean, well, I'm old enough for Coke now, so I wondered... I mean, you don't have to, but...

MALE: Okay, baby girl. Okay. Let's tell that story too, why not? So. Okay. So Daddy Luke and I got married – they changed the law, made it so boys could marry boys, so we got married. We'd lived together for a while. And... well, Daddy Rob had been sick...

CHILD: Was it the same as what James had?

MALE: No, love. No. Daddy Rob... I just... I was very

sad, for a long time, after James. And then after the burglary, I got very sad again. And scared, all the time. About everything. Everything and nothing. Daddy Luke helped a lot with that. He made me feel better. Safer. Eventually I felt well enough that we talked about having a child. We'd both always wanted one. And... well, Charley, you know that two boys can't make a baby?

CHILD: Um.

MALE: Oh, kiddo. I'm sorry. I'm sorry. We really should have said. We thought... well we were waiting for you to be old enough...

CHILD: I am old enough! I know babies grow in women's bellies!

MALE: Right. That's exactly right. So, the way it works is, a man and a woman make a baby, then it grows in the woman's belly, then the baby is born.

CHILD: So... but... only one man? So, you and Daddy Luke didn't both make me?

MALE: No, sweet pea. Just Daddy Luke.

CHILD: But...

MALE: Listen. Listen. Daddy Rob loves you to the moon and back. I'm your Daddy. Just like Daddy Luke. But I couldn't... We went to the doctors, to make sure we were both healthy, would make a healthy baby, and I... well, there was something wrong and I couldn't. I wanted to, believe me, baby girl, I wanted to, but I couldn't.

CHILD: So… but…

MALE: It's okay, baby girl. It's okay. Come here. Come here.

CHILD: I'm okay, Daddy Rob. I'm okay. It's just… a lot.

MALE: It is. It is a lot. Are you okay? Do you want to stop? Do you want me to stop?

CHILD: Is there more? More story?

MALE: There's more, yes. But only if you want it.

CHILD: I do, Daddy Rob. I mean, I do want to know the rest of the story.

MALE: Okay. So, anyway, we still knew we wanted to make a baby. So… well… You know Auntie Sally?

CHILD: Yeah. I love Auntie Sally!

MALE: I know you do, kiddo. She loves you too. Anyway…

CHILD: I love Auntie Jo, too. I mean, I love both of them.

MALE: I know, sweet pea. It's okay. Anyway, so Auntie Sally agreed to make a baby for Daddy Luke and Daddy Rob.

CHILD: So… Daddy Luke made a baby with Auntie Sally?

MALE: …Yeah. Yes. They made you. Daddy Luke and Auntie Sally. And when she had you, Auntie Sally gave you to me and Daddy Luke to be our little girl forever and ever.

CHILD: So… does that mean Auntie Sally is my mummy?

MALE: Yes. Yes, she is. Is that okay?

CHILD: Oh! Oh yeah, it's fine! I mean, I do love her, so...

MALE: I know you do.

CHILD: Can I call her mummy, when I see her?

MALE: *<sigh>* Well, probably, but I need to finish the story first, okay?

CHILD: Okay! Sure!

MALE: Thank you. So, anyway, they made you, and Daddy Rob and Daddy Luke have raised you, and we love you, and we're very proud of you. You're our shining star. You know that?

CHILD: Of course I do, I mean, you always tell me.

MALE: Good. Because here's where the story gets a little bit scary. Like in a fairy tale. When there's a wicked witch or something. So I need you to be brave, now. Can you be brave for me?

CHILD: I can be brave, Daddy Rob. You can tell me.

MALE: Okay. okay. Well, you remember me telling you about the bombs? The big ones?

CHILD: That gave you nightmares?

MALE: Yes. Them.

CHILD: Yeah.

MALE: Okay. Well, here's the thing. You remember the big bang that knocked the power out? That broke all the windows?

CHILD: Yes.

MALE: It was one of the bombs.

CHILD: Really?
MALE: I'm afraid so, yes. I know it was.
CHILD: It... but... How can you tell?
MALE: Lots of reasons. The brightness of the blast. The way I got burns on my legs. The dust in the rain. The... the birds. The dead birds.
CHILD: The bomb killed the birds?
MALE: Well, yes. Basically. I mean, it's not just the bomb. The bombs... they have a kind of poison in them. In the explosion, I mean. And it gets up into the air, and it kills... it poisons the animals.
CHILD: Is that why Mr Scribbles died?
MALE: Yes.
CHILD: That makes me so sad...
MALE: Oh, I know...
CHILD: It's not fair, Daddy Rob...
MALE: I know, baby girl, I know, come here, come here, have a daddy cuddle. Come on.
CHILD: It's just so sad.
MALE: I know. I know. But, okay, so listen. The poison, it's in the air, it's all around but...
CHILD: Daddy Rob?
MALE: Please just listen, okay? You remember George's Marvellous Medicine? We read it, remember?
CHILD: Yes! With the mean old lady!
MALE: That's right! Well, pumpkin, we're going to make our own version of the medicine to protect us from the poison.

CHILD: Really?

MALE: Really. We're going to make a medicine so strong that it'll make us sleep, like in Sleeping Beauty, and when we wake up, we'll be all better and...

CHILD: And Daddy Luke will wake us up with a kiss!

MALE: That's right, baby girl. That's exactly right.

CHILD: Oh, Daddy Rob, that makes me so happy! Can we do it now? How can we?

MALE: Well, you're going to need to be very brave. Like the princess in the story?

CHILD: With the bow and arrow? And the bear?

MALE: Yeah.

CHILD: I can be brave, Daddy Rob.

MALE: I know you can, sweetheart. I know you can. Listen, here's what I need you to do. I need you to go into Sharon and Pete's house...

CHILD: Like we did before?

MALE: Like that, yes. But I need you to go up into the upstairs bathroom.

CHILD: Why?

MALE: Because I need you to get all of the medicine they have in their medicine cupboard.

CHILD: Why?

MALE: Because we're making marvellous medicine, remember?

CHILD: Why?

MALE: So we can sleep until all the poison has gone and we're all better.

CHILD: Why?

MALE: Because... Ah, you little noodle head, you got me!

CHILD: *<laughs>*

MALE: Listen, though, this is important. I need you to be the brave one. I can't go in there myself, my leg hurts too much. Can you do it?

CHILD: I think so, Daddy Rob.

MALE: Good girl. Here, get that carrier bag, over there.

CHILD: It's got things in it, Daddy Rob.

MALE: It's just bike pumps, tip them out.

<clattering noises>

Good girl. Good girl. Now, I want you to put all the pills you can find in here, okay? All the medicine bottles.

CHILD: Where will they be, Daddy Rob?

MALE: In the bathroom. The upstairs one. You know our cabinet? With the mirror slidey doors?

CHILD: Oh! Yes, of course!

MALE: Like that. Or it may have handles to pull. I don't know. You'll have to see.

CHILD: Okay.

MALE: Stand on the toilet if you can't reach, okay? Be careful.

CHILD: Okay, Daddy Rob.

MALE: Okay. And Charley? All the pills. In packets, in jars, anything, if it's a tablet put it in the bag.

CHILD: Okay, Daddy Rob.

MALE: Good girl...

CHILD: Daddy Rob, I'm really scared! I don't want to do it!

MALE: Oh, baby girl, princess, come here, come here lovely, shh, shh, it's okay, you're okay, shh, listen, it's just like being a princess in a story, okay? You're the brave princess, going on a quest to get the magic potion, okay?

CHILD: The Marvellous Medicine!

MALE: Right! Right, the marvellous medicine. And listen, baby girl, I'm sorry, okay? I really am. I'd do it myself if I could, but Daddy Rob's leg is so poorly, I couldn't make it up the stairs...

CHILD: ...and plus you're all hot, Daddy Rob.

MALE: I am, poppet, yeah. Running a temperature, I think.

CHILD: Because of the poison?

MALE: Well, and my hurty leg, yes.

CHILD: And the medicine will make you all better? Your leg, even?

MALE: I think it will, yes.

CHILD: Well, I guess it is Marvellous Medicine, after all!

MALE: Exactly! Exactly. So, Charley, I really need you to go now, okay?

CHILD: But... what if the men come back, Daddy Rob?

MALE: They won't. I promise they won't.

CHILD: How do you know…?

MALE: Charley! Because I do, okay? Because… Because the poison will have made them too sick, okay? They were out and walking about in it all the time, and now they will be too ill to come back, okay?

CHILD: Are you sure, Daddy Rob?

MALE: Super sure. All the sure.

CHILD: I'm still scared, Daddy Rob.

MALE: I know, little girl. I know. But you're brave too, aren't you? That's right. Daddy Rob's brave one. You can do it, I know you can. Okay? The sooner you go, the sooner you can come back, okay?

CHILD: Okay, Daddy Rob.

MALE: Okay. Can you manage the door okay?

CHILD: Yes, of course!

MALE: Okay great. Leave it open, okay? So I can hear you if you need me.

CHILD: I will be fine, Daddy Rob.

MALE: I know you will, darling. Good girl. Straight to the bathroom, all the pills in the bag, straight back. Okay?

CHILD: And then we make the Marvellous Medicine?

MALE: Then we make the medicine!

CHILD: Okay.

MALE: Okay.

CHILD: Okay, Daddy Rob. I will be back before you know it.

MALE: Okay.

<door opening, footsteps, fading>

Don't. Don't you judge me. Don't you fucking dare. I have to do this, now. I have to. Leg is fucking broken. The pain is like nothing else. And anyway, the way my foot is swollen, it's got to be blood poisoning. I don't have long. Less than a day, probably, when I can still think straight. She's already started with the nausea. I'll be dead in two or three days, and useless for most of it. I'm not putting her through that. I can't. I won't. Leave her alive, alone? I can't. I just fucking can't.

<sobbing>

I'm sorry. I'm so sorry. I didn't have a choice, about any of this. I didn't ask for it. And now... I just want it to be over. We've had our time. There's no coming back. I've been a shitty dad, in a lot of ways, but I'm not going to let her down, not on this one, not...

<crying>

Oh, shit shit shit. Fuck. Okay. Okay. Listen. Whoever you are, listen. Okay? I know you made it, okay? I know humans are going to make it back here someday. I can't imagine exactly who you are, how hard your life is. Has been. Or how easy. I know you're out there. Sorry about the mess. Bit of a state. But listen, okay? We were here. Okay? We were here. Charley and Luke and I, we were all here. We lived, in this painfully middle class estate. We made a home, together. We loved and laughed and argued and drank and made love and made a family. Charley, she… fuck, she could have been anything. Bright kid. Wilful little shit. You've heard her. You know. She could have been anything. Fuck, she was something. We were something. This is what you forget, I think. This is what blinds you. Eyes on the horizon all the fucking time, worrying about how everything is going to turn out. It's bollocks. Clearly. There's now, and that's it.

I miss my husband. I miss him so much. I miss my mum and dad. I hope it was quick, for all of them. I'm sure it was.

And you. I hope… I hope you're okay. I hope that things are okay, or good. I hope you have clean water and medicine and movies and music. Dancing. I hope you dance. You should. You should.

We existed, okay? We lived. Raise a glass to that. Raise a glass to us. To life and those that lived it. I know this'll be a ghost town for a long time, but if you're hearing this, you've come back. I hope that's right. I hope people get to live here again.

I hope my little girl makes it back soon.

When she does, I'm gonna use what she's found. Hopefully they've got some proper painkillers, tranqs, something like that. I think I'll melt the chocolate, mix the powder in with it. That should mask the taste. Plus it'll seem like fun, like a treat.

God, Charley, I'm sorry. I'm so sorry. I know staying here was right, that the dose we took was way too strong, but still. Ah, fuck, this is shit. This is so shit.

Please come back soon, little girl. Please find something we can use. I'm sorry I won't see the woman you were going to be, but it's been an honour to be your father. You are my whole world. You are perfect. Perfect. I can't...

CHILD: Daddy Rob!

MALE: Yes! Baby girl?

CHILD: I found loads! Loads!

MALE: Good girl, bring the bag in here. Goodbye.

CHILD: Who are you saying goodbye to?

<ends>

Kit Power lives in Milton Keynes, and writes about what scares him. His novel *GodBomb!*, novella collection *Breaking Point*, and short story collection *A WARNING ABOUT YOUR FUTURE ENSLAVEMENT THAT YOU WILL DISMISS AS A COLLECTION OF SHORT FICTION AND ESSAYS BY KIT POWER* are all available now. A non-fiction book on the Ken Russell/The Who movie *Tommy* is forthcoming from PS Publishing, as part of their acclaimed Midnight Monograph series.

Kit also blogs and reviews for Ginger Nuts of Horror, including his five-years-and-counting 'My Life In Horror' project, and a first read and review of all of Brian Keene's published work, both of which are ongoing. In all his spare time, he podcasts, plays *Magic: The Gathering Arena*, and tries to be a good father and husband.

www.patreon.com/kitpower

Made in the USA
Monee, IL
02 January 2023

24276650R00097